Aberration

Aberration

by

Steven P. Marini

† † † †

Gypsy Shadow Publishing

Aberration
A Jack Contino Crime Story
by
Steven P. Marini

Gypsy Shadow Publishing, LLC.
Lockhart, TX
www.gypsyshadow.com

Library of Congress Control Number: 2013944634

eBook ISBN: 978-1-61950-167-6
Print ISBN: 978-1-61950-168-3

Published in the United States of America

First eBook Edition: July, 2013
First Print Edition: July, 2013

DEDICATION

To my real family and to my new family of readers. May
you both grow in number.

Aberration: . . . mental irregularity or disorder, esp. of a
minor nature;
lapse from a sound mental state.

Prologue

I needed a stiff drink.

Cape Cod, the premier vacation spot in New England, was my new home. I was supposed to be able to relax here, live life in the slow lane and not get shot again. My days as a Boston cop were over. Leave the Winter Hill boys and the Boston Mob to younger men. Join the Dennis Police. With my pension from the Metropolitan District Commission Police, known as the METs, and a full salary from Dennis, I nearly doubled my income. Nat's salary as a nurse was gravy. We could slide.

I was the Chief of Detectives on the Dennis, Massachusetts PD, but I was the only detective on the Dennis PD, so I didn't catch any crap from subordinates. I told Natalie I'd have to work late, checking on a housebreak in Dennis. Told her not to make dinner for me, that I'd grab a bite someplace. It took over an hour to wrap things up at the crime scene. Afterward, I needed some time to myself.

I stopped at a little place near home in Yarmouth at about eight o'clock, and parked a few rows back in the lot. No need to have my car easily spotted near the door. Just a precaution. As you entered, Goodfellows was a sports bar on the left side, a diner on the right. It was a hole in the wall, but the food was great. You could get as good a steak or prime rib here as any of the big name restaurants in the mid-Cape region.

So why did I feel so uptight? The belly wound that almost killed me a couple of years before gave me some pain once in a while, but after, was it three years?—hell, I could handle it. It wasn't the pain. It was the memory. That scum Secani put a round into me before I could react. Was I getting too old, too slow?

Maybe Nat was right. Maybe I should give up police work. But I just couldn't. Too many bastards out there just had to break the law. They needed to be stopped. Too many assholes making life harder for innocent people. Too many shits like Tommy Shea, who needed to have their luck run out. But on the Cape it was supposed to be easier. I was supposed to be able to take it slow, and I was trying to. So why did I get so damned wound up sometimes?

I navigated my way to a stool away from the door, on the far left and just around the bar's corner. From there, I could see the door and the whole room, left and right. Perfect.

"Jim Beam, rocks," I said when the bartender came around.

"Got it. Name's Jack, right? I've seen you in here before. We chatted a little. You're with the Dennis PD, right?"

"Right."

He looked at me, eye to eye, then he shifted his gaze to my sport coat.

"So, Jack, you're carrying now, right?" he said.

I sat up straight. "That's procedure. I'm on my way home."

"No problem, Jack," he said. "I just figured, you know?"

There was a full house on the diner side, a few couples and some guys my age wearing ballplayer's uniforms. Senior Softball league guys. Pretty cool, those old bastards still playing a boys' game and running around the bases. Still drinking pitchers of beer after a game. Good for them. Better to get a strained hamstring than a bullet.

The bartender brought me the bourbon, setting it down on a napkin in front of me.

"What's your name again?" I asked.

"Barry. Barry Morgan." He smiled.

Barry was in his mid-forties, I'd guess. He was about six feet and had a decent build, fairly strong and not much gut. His hair was brown and thick, no signs of gray yet.

"Enjoy your drink, Jack," he said and walked away.

I enjoyed it all right. Then I enjoyed another.

After two good ones, it was time to go home.

I pulled into the driveway around eight-thirty. A guy my size has a tough time entering the house quietly, so I didn't try. But I'm not a door slammer, either.

Nat was reading in the living room, sitting in a recliner near a floor light. I strode up to her, bent down and gave her

2

a smooch on the cheek, stumbling a little and grabbing the back of her chair for balance.

"Hi, hon, you okay?" she said.

"Yeah, yeah, I just lost my balance."

"You ate, I guess."

"Yes, I grabbed a bite on the way home."

"And some bourbon, I guess."

"I had a couple with dinner, that's all."

Nat didn't respond to that. She just got up from the chair, folded her book and laid it on the table beside her chair. "I'm going to bed, Jack." She started to walk to the stairs but stopped, turned and came up to me. "Was it a bad day, Jack?"

"I've had worse and I've had better," I said. "Thanks for asking." I took Nat in my arms and gave her a big hug, lifting her off her feet. She felt great in my arms. I held her like that for a few seconds, then let her down slowly. "Don't worry, hon, tomorrow will be better, I'm sure. It'll be Friday. Things get better for everybody on Friday. You wait and see."

Chapter One

I was standing in front of the bathroom mirror, running my finger over the scar across my chin. It had faded somewhat, but I saw it every day, a reminder of Tommy Shea, who put it there with a shard of glass a long time ago. That was a score I needed to settle. Then the phone rang, disturbing my Friday night.

I was hoping for a peaceful summer weekend. I should have known better. Cape Cod is the top beach vacation area in Massachusetts and the population explodes every summer, way beyond its year-round number, thanks to all the summer residents and weekend warriors. Dennis is a small town right in the middle of the Cape and my current place of employment, Chief of Detectives, Dennis Police Department. A murder had taken place at a Dennis restaurant.

Natalie and I had bought a three bedroom Cape style house in West Yarmouth, just west of Dennis, so it would take me about twenty minutes to get to the scene. I dressed, told Nat about the call and headed out.

I arrived at the Beachgoer just before midnight. The Dennis officers and two State Police had set up a perimeter and were routing traffic. I was directed by the officers to the rear parking lot. A young man sat slumped in the driver's seat of an old black sedan. His arms hung by his sides and his head was tilted forward, his chin into his chest like someone grabbing a nap in a chair. I hadn't seen so much blood in a long time, since my days with the METs. Some gangland killings were done with knives or broken bottles applied to the throat. This wound looked clean and straight across.

I talked to the uniformed officers who were examining the scene. "What do you think, a drug deal gone bad?"

"Could be. There's a letter-sized envelope on the front passenger seat. It could have been money or drugs in it."

I checked the contents of the envelope on the front passenger seat and saw the money, one hundred dollars. That ruled out robbery as a motive. I jotted down some notes into a small pad and then went into the building to find Pearson. He stood up when he saw me enter the room. Sergeant Jim Pearson was a veteran officer, about six-foot-one and built like a linebacker. He was a good cop and I liked him right from the time I started in Dennis.

The restaurant had the usual nautical décor, typical of a Cape Cod establishment. The bar caught my eye, though. It was short and L-shaped, made of shiny mahogany with a deep finish. The bar stools were wood with red vinyl over padding. I could enjoy a good drink at a bar like this one.

"Hello, Jack," he said. "This is Ed Conley and his wife, Betsy, and son, Billy." Billy was about sixteen, short and thin, wearing jeans and a yellow T-shirt. Betsy was tall and thin, with light brown hair. She wore a black skirt, white blouse and white earrings.

"They're the owners of the restaurant and the ones who found the victim." He then turned to Ed Conley. "This is Detective Contino. He'll be conducting the investigation."

"Jim, when the Assistant D.A. arrives, tell him I'll talk to him as soon as I've interviewed the Conleys."

I reached out my hand toward Ed and we exchanged a polite handshake as Sergeant Pearson walked away. I sat down and flipped my notepad open on the table.

"I know this must be very difficult for you, so I'll only take a few minutes tonight, but I need to get as much fresh information as you can give me."

The Conley family nodded simultaneously.

"Mr. Conley, there's an envelope with one hundred dollars in it on the front passenger seat. Do you know anything about that?"

"Yes," said Ed. "I pay Manny a cash bonus now and then. That's what's in the envelope. I paid him a bonus tonight."

I nodded and made a note. "What's his full name, please?"

"It's Manny Duarte."

"What time did he and the other help leave?"

"I dismissed the waitresses first, just after eleven. I asked Manny to wait a few minutes so I could pay him his

5

bonus. I don't want to do it in front of the girls, because I don't want them to think he's getting special treatment. They get their tips and do pretty well with that. This isn't much of a drinking joint, so the bartender doesn't get much in the way of tips. Manny never complains and he doesn't rob the till, so I take care of him."

I made more notes and continued questioning. "So the waitresses left first and Manny hung around awhile, is that right?"

Ed nodded. "Yes. He went into the restroom first. When he came out, I gave him his bonus."

"How many waitresses are there?"

Betsy spoke up. "Just two. DeeDee O'Hare and Millie Wallenski."

"How did they get along with Manny?"

Betsy shrugged. "They all seemed to get along fine."

"Okay, that's good. I'll need to be able to get in touch with them. Do you have their home addresses and phones?"

"Manny lived with his parents in Dennisport. I feel so bad for them. I'll get their information for you and the girls' addresses, too," said Betsy. She rose slowly from the table and went into the small office off the side of the kitchen.

"Ed, please try to tell me what happened tonight."

"Okay, Detective. I do the cooking and Billy runs the dishwasher during the summer. I had just finished cleaning up the kitchen and came out to the bar. I was having a glass of water and last call had passed, so I dimmed the lights to send a message to the remaining patrons to drink up and move on. As the last customers went out the door, I dismissed Manny and the waitresses. They made no offer to stay late for cleanup. Betsy, Billy and I would take care of that as well as cash out the register. Betsy is the receptionist and restaurant cashier and Manny took care of the bar. Manny was a rare find. Tonight was his bonus night, so I asked him to wait a minute after the women left. Manny smiled whenever I said that to him.

"Manny took the envelope with five twenty dollar bills in it from Betsy, thanked us and walked out through the kitchen to the back door leading to the dirt parking lot. I asked the employees to always park out back. Billy powered up the vacuum cleaner and we started cleaning up the place. A little after midnight we were done.

"I told Billy to go start up the car. You know how Cape Cod air can be cool at night. I like to have Billy warm up the engine for a few minutes."

I looked at Billy. "What happened next, Billy?"

The boy was calm in answering. "I was surprised to see Manny's car still there, with Manny sitting behind the wheel, so I jogged up to it to see what he was up to. The window was opened so I called to him. I wondered what he was doing here. He didn't answer. He just sat there. When I got up close I could tell something was wrong. Manny was sitting with his head down. There was blood everywhere."

"What happened next?"

Ed answered, "Billy called out to me for help. He said Manny was in his car and maybe dead. It was awful. I told Betsy to call the police right away and told Billy to stay with his mom."

"And you checked out Manny?"

"Yes. I approached the car and called to him. I stopped when I saw the heavy amount of blood on Manny's shirt just below the collar. There's a flood light on the roof, but there wasn't enough light shining on Manny inside his car for me to get a clear look, so I got a flashlight in the restaurant and went back to look again. I flashed the light on Manny and got a better look. I wish I hadn't. Manny's throat had been cut halfway around his neck. The police cars got here within a few minutes. Sergeant Pearson told us to wait inside while they checked things out."

I looked back toward Ed and asked if the waitresses were gone by the time Manny left the building. Ed assured me that they were, emphasizing that these were young women whose nights began when they went off duty. They were always in a hurry to get going after work. If the waitresses left in a rush, they probably didn't see anything happen in the parking lot, but I'd have to talk to them just the same.

"Okay, just a little bit more." I took a short breath while looking at my notes. "What can you tell me about Manny? How well did you know him?"

"He's a nice young man, well, was," said Ed. "He started working with us in June after graduating from the community college. He went into the army after high school, did a tour in Nam and went to Four Cs full time after that. He majored in Hospitality Management and wanted to learn the restaurant business from the bottom up. He was proud to have gone to community college, the first in his family, he said, to get an education. They're Cape Verdean. He was born and raised here on Cape Cod. What a shame! He was a great kid. I was hoping he would be working with us for a long time."

Betsy returned with the addresses and phone numbers for DeeDee, Millie and Manny's parents. I took the slip of paper, folded it and put it in my shirt pocket.

"Thanks. That'll be all for now. You can close up and go home. Get some rest. The officers will finish up outside at the car. They won't have to come into the building again. Goodnight."

Ed nodded to me as he got up to leave. I heard Betsy speak to him.

"Ed, what are we going to do?" Her voice was cracking.

"We'll shut down tomorrow," he said. "I don't see what else we can do. I'll check with a temp agency for a bartender. We'll reopen as soon as we can. Let's go home."

I walked back to Manny's car and told Sergeant Pearson to wait for the medical examiner to arrive for the body. Pearson had already called the contract towing company so the car could be towed to the police station once Manny's body was removed from it.

"Jim, I need you to inform the parents. I'll check on the two waitresses tonight. Tell his parents that I'll be calling on them tomorrow."

I gave Jim the contact information for the Duarte family. We both had experience notifying next of kin with news of a death. It never gets easy. Neither does the follow-up in a homicide. That would be my job.

Chapter Two

I tried DeeDee O'Hare's residence, but it was empty. I guess she was out partying with her pals, so I went to find Millie Wallenski.

I reached her place and knocked on the door. A high-pitched voice answered. "Who is it?"

My voice gets deeper late in the day, adding some tone of authority, I guess. "Dennis Police. I'd like to speak with Millie Wallenski, please."

She opened the door.

She was tiny and a bit chubby, with short brown hair. She was barefoot, wearing cut-off sweat pants and a blue T-shirt hanging loose over her cut-offs. Millie's eyes opened wide at the sight of me. At six-four and two-hundred-thirty pounds, I was twice her size: a tall, husky, middle-aged man in tan slacks, a yellow shirt with open collar and a Navy blue blazer. I was probably as old, or older, than her parents, so she certainly didn't see this as a summer social opportunity.

"What's wrong, officer?"

"I'm Detective Jack Contino, of the Dennis Police, Miss. May I come in?"

"Yes, of course." She stepped back into the living room. She saw my eyes go to the pizza and beer on the end table next to the easy chair and she quickly ran to it and grabbed the napkin beside the paper pizza plate. She realized that she had pizza sauce on her mouth, and she wiped it off thoroughly.

"Are you Millie Wallenski?"

"Yes, I am." Millie stood in front of her chair. "What seems to be the problem, Detective?"

"Perhaps you'd better sit down, Miss Wallenski."

"No, I'm okay. What is it?" The worry began to show on her face.

"You work at the Beachgoer Restaurant, correct?"
Millie nodded.

"The bartender, Manny Duarte, was murdered there tonight, in the parking lot right after work."

Millie's eyes and mouth opened wide and she brought both her hands up to her mouth. As she felt her knees grow weak, she lowered herself into the chair. "Oh, my God! What happened?"

"His throat was cut while he was sitting in his car."

"Ohhhhh." She edged further back into the chair. "No, no!" Her eyes began to fill with tears, realizing that this was really happening.

I knew that there were times when a big cop could be pretty intimidating, especially to someone not accustomed to dealing with the police. This must have been such a time for Millie Wallenski, so I sat down on the sofa near her to minimize the intimidation. I spoke softly. "Tell me when you last saw Manny."

Millie wiped away her tears and grabbed her napkin again to blow her nose. She held onto the napkin, crushing it in her hands as she struggled to regain her voice.

"When I got off duty, just after eleven. He was still in the restaurant near the bar when DeeDee and I walked out. She's the other waitress." Her voice had a tremor in it. "I think Mr. Conley was going to pay him his bonus, so he had to stay around. We all know he gets a bonus, but Mr. Conley always waits until we leave before he pays him. We understand."

"DeeDee is DeeDee O'Hare, is that right?"
Millie nodded her head. "Yes."

"What did she do when you left?"

Millie tried to bring her thoughts together. "Well, she ran across the parking lot to her car and drove away kinda quick."

"She was in a hurry?"

"I guess so. It's Friday night and she goes off to join her friends. She has a boyfriend named Jared and they pal around with her house mate, Judy Black, and her guy. She's a real party girl."

"Miss Wallenski, let's back up a bit. I know this is hard, but I really need you to help me. Take your time and try to tell me what went on in the Beachgoer tonight."

She wiped her face with her hand and took a breath. "Okay, I'll try." Her weeping died down.

She told me DeeDee was about five foot-three, short blond hair and was looking great in her short black hot pants and long sleeved white blouse and that Manny Duarte couldn't take his eyes off her. He almost dropped some pilsner glasses at the beer tap. DeeDee knew he was staring at her but she didn't let on. She just went about her business. Manny kept watching her. Millie told him to put his eyes back in his head at one point and she reminded him that DeeDee was spoken for this summer. Manny just laughed. DeeDee heard him laugh and wanted to know what the joke was all about.

"Did Manny ever ask her out?"

"Not that I know of."

I guessed that Millie was in her late twenties, much older than most of the summer set on the Cape. But there were people in their twenties who had jobs that let them keep the summer dream alive. Millie told me she was an elementary school teacher who spent her summers working on Cape Cod, as she had been doing since she was a college student. After five years of teaching school, she was still unattached and so she continued to spend her summers at her parent's cottage in Dennisport, a stone's throw from the Beachgoer. Her parents came down to the Cape on weekends, so Millie had a friend of hers, another unattached teacher from her school, join her during the summer.

The Beachgoer was known for food more than drink. It had no live entertainment. The kitchen closed at ten and the bar stayed open until eleven. For the few in the after ten crowd, it served as a warm up for the late night bar hoppers and partygoers.

"Do you know the names of her friends, Miss Wallenski?"

"Her boyfriend's name is Jared something. He works at the Chicken Roost, a little restaurant near here on Lower County. There's a bunch of kids in their crowd. I don't know them by name. Sometimes I see them on the beach together. DeeDee talks about Jared a lot, so I know his name."

"There was no one at her rental house. I was just there."

"Well, they're probably still out at a watering hole. Probably will close the joint."

11

I checked my watch. It was twenty-to-one, so they still had some drinking time before last call. *No point in going back to O'Hare's place now. I'll check in on her in the morning.*

"Miss Wallenski, what else do you know about the victim, anything about his friends, his enemies?"

"I only knew him at work." She was still sobbing. "I never saw him other than that, except once at the beach. Everybody at work seemed to like him. He was always friendly, you know. Who would want to kill him?"

I took a business card out of my pocket and handed it to Millie. "That's all for now, Miss Wallenski. If you think of anything or hear anything that relates to this incident, call me any time of the day or night."

"Yes, of course," replied Millie.

I was spent by the time I got home, but felt too on edge to go right to bed. I kicked off my shoes, draped my coat over a kitchen chair and poured a bourbon over ice, a double. In the living room, I settled into a recliner, pushing it back so that the footrest sprang out in front. It was wind-down time from this night's work. One drink wouldn't do the trick. *I'll go for two.*

I'd almost dropped off to sleep in the chair when Natalie came into the room.

"Was it very bad, Jack?"

"Damn it, hon, I didn't mean to wake you. Sorry."

"You didn't wake me. I was never asleep, just reading. You know how it goes when you get those late night calls."

We'd been through nights like this many times over the years.

"At least, Nat, this time there were no gun fights with drug dealers or Boston bad guys. It was nasty, though, a young man's neck was slit while he sat in his car after work. I guess you've seen stuff like that when you worked as an emergency room nurse."

Nat looked down for a second. "Yes, especially when I worked at Mass General. I suppose I can't persuade you to throw that drink away. If that old gut wound is acting up, it's not the best thing for you."

"I'm fine, Nat, really. I can handle it."

"Then you won't mind if I join you. Don't get up, Jack. I'll fix it myself."

I got up anyway and moved over to the sofa so there would be room for Nat to sit with me when she got her drink. We snuggled in and I told her more about the case. She was the best medicine a guy could have. It's always good to have a couple of drinks with my gal.

Chapter Three

"Tora lora lora loo,
They're looking for monkeys up at the zoo.
And says I: "If I had a face like you
I'd join the British army."

The audience at The Irish Pub whooped and hollered their approval as the band ended their set with the chorus to an old traditional Irish tune. Once a song of rebellion, it now served mostly as a drinking song. All ethnic groups enjoyed it, but those of Irish descent sang it with added gusto.

Freddy Marcellino was one of DeeDee and Jared's friends. He waved his hand high in the air when he saw Jared Wilkes and Scott Seldon, Judy Black's boyfriend, walk through the door, getting Jared's attention and directing him to the bar. The two late-comers smiled and joined their friends. DeeDee was flirting with Freddy in a drunken giggle. Jared was amused at the scene.

"Hi Jared," called the bartender. They had become acquainted that summer since Jared had been to the Irish Pub several times with his friends. Since he was the bartender at The Chicken Roost restaurant, he liked to introduce himself to fellow bartenders.

"Hey Rusty," replied Jared. "Two Chivas rocks, please." Jared took a twenty out of his pocket and rolled it up between his long fingers. When their drinks arrived, he slipped it to Rusty and told him to keep the change. Rusty unrolled the bill and smiled.

"Thanks, Jared." Jared had a habit of giving generous tips to bartenders. Rusty acted as if it was nothing unusual.

"Well, look uze 'ere," said DeeDee, finally noticing her lover's presence. She suddenly wrapped both her arms around Freddy and purred in his ear. "Freddy, ol' boy, I'm 'fraid is over between uz. This 'ansome stud 'ere has claimed my hand, not to mention my azz, in the state of faithful shacking upingness."

"And it's a fine state you're in," replied Freddy. "Unhand me, woman, whilst I drown my sorrows."

Jared smiled and shook his head in disbelief. He had seen Dee get a buzz on before, but he'd never seen her get this drunk. You'd think she was celebrating a special event.

He watched DeeDee move next to Bob Lenox at the bar and poked his shoulder. As he turned toward her, she sang to him, "An' if I has a faze lik YOOOOOO, I'd join a British army." She broke into laughter and slapped him on the chest. Freddy, standing on her other side, laughed and sipped his beer. Bob rolled his eyes at both of them.

"You know DeeDee, you gotta cheer up," said Freddy. "I hate to see you so depressed."

DeeDee spun around, poked her finger into his chest and tried to repeat the song to him. "An' if I has a faz like YOOOOOO . . ." Her loud laugh interrupted her singing, and Freddy raised his hand to guard against her giggle spray. Jared knew DeeDee wouldn't be driving home tonight.

"Freddy, keep an eye on her while I hit the head," said Jared, and he strolled away to the men's room.

"Will do, Jared. Now DeeDee, try to behave yourself."

She giggled into her drink.

A young Black man approached the bar, stopping beside DeeDee. He wore a gray T-shirt that said U MASS on the front, cutoff blue jeans and brown loafers on his athletic frame and stood a shade under six feet. He gazed up and down at DeeDee's figure. "Say, happy girl, care to dance?"

"Ah, hold on," said Freddy. "The young woman is spoken for."

DeeDee spun her head toward Freddy. "Oh, hell, a danze is juzz a danze. 'Sides, Jared's a johnner, fer now." She turned to the Black man. "Yez, letz hop to it, Mr. Bojingles." She took his hand and led him to the crowded dance floor.

"Mr. Bojangles, huh? That's cute, happy girl."

DeeDee laughed and slapped the man on the chest. "I like you, Bojugels. You're cute." She danced up close to him, turned and rubbed her ass against his thigh and stumbled. The man grabbed her around the waist to keep her from falling. She spun toward him and threw her arms around his neck. "Ooooh. Hah, hah. Nize move. Almose got a good feely, din ya? Hah." She backed away a step, still dancing.

Jared returned to the bar next to Freddy. "Where's DeeDee? Did she pass out somewhere?"

"Not yet. She's out there." He pointed to the dance floor.

Jared spotted his girlfriend dancing with the young Black man. He stretched his neck and stood straight up. "What the fuck."

The song ended and DeeDee grabbed the Black man's hand again and pulled him to the bar next to her friends. "Hey Jared, y'ole stud. Thiz iz Mr. Bogangles. We're danzin."

"Not anymore," said Jared and he grabbed DeeDee's hand away from the Black man. "This dance is over. This is The Irish Pub. They don't have jungle drums in here."

The Black man lost his smile, and he stepped toward Jared.

As he did, Freddy jumped between them. "Cool your jets, guys. Nobody's looking for trouble. Besides, I think we were just about to leave."

Jared stood rigid.

The Black man relaxed his posture and exhaled softly, as if he had been holding it before exploding. He looked at Jared, nodding his head, as if to say *there'll be another time.* He went back to his friends several tables away. They had risen to their feet while watching the exchange with Jared, but they sat back down as the young man approached, waving his palms downward.

DeeDee draped herself on Freddy and giggled. "Way to go, Freddy, the peeze maker."

Scott sipped his drink while Dee separated herself from Freddy and draped her body onto Jared's, moving like a chimp swinging from tree to tree. She put her glass on the bar and turned toward Jared. She wrapped her arms around him and snuggled up, putting her head against his chest, as if she were climbing into an upright bed.

"Oh-oh," said Jared, looking at Freddy. "I think this gal is running on empty."

Freddy shook his head, holding his drink up to his mouth. "Well, she blew her chance to take advantage of me. You'll have to handle her from here on, Jared."

"I'll do my best," he replied. "Time to go."

The bunch went into the parking lot and then the group splintered apart as they headed for their cars. Freddy and Bob each had one and Judy Black, DeeDee's housemate, had driven to the Pub on her own. Jared extracted DeeDee's keys from a pocket in her tight shorts, and Judy kissed Scott before going to her car. The two couples headed to the gals' rented house while Bob and Freddy drove off to their own place. It was wind-down time.

The happy time was near its end.

Chapter Four

Saturday morning came too quickly. I slept well. Fatigue from the late night and a couple of stiff drinks helped. I would have preferred not to have to go to headquarters today. With a murder investigation in progress, however, I could look forward to an unenjoyable summer Saturday on the Cape.

I was supposed to be getting away from murder and mayhem. That's why I'd retired from the METs, after thirty plus years of service. The bullet I took in the gut a few years earlier nearly finished me, so Nat started urging me to quit. I wasn't ready to hang it up, so when I learned about the job opening on the Dennis PD, I persuaded Nat that working on the Cape would be calm and easy, nothing like the stuff in Boston. She went for it. Our grown-up kids could come and visit and maybe I'd take up sailing, something I always wanted to do.

We moved to West Yarmouth in 1977, and the first year was just what we wanted. But this case, in August 1978, seemed like old times.

I entered the police headquarters through the front entrance, smiled at the desk officer and proceeded to the office area. It was behind a solid wall, through a door with smoked glass on the top half. I smelled the fresh coffee as soon as I entered the office. Jim Pearson sat at a desk dressed in civvies, sipping the coffee he had just made and looking at an open file folder in front of him.

I made my way to the coffee pot and filled a Styrofoam cup with coffee and condiments. "What are you doing here today, Jim?"

"I don't plan to stay long. Something about that killing last night rang a bell and I wanted to check on it before I let myself start enjoying the weekend."

"I'm glad to see such dedication in the case. Makes me feel less alone on a Saturday morning. Thanks for notifying the parents."

"No problem, Jack. I know you've been there before. You've got the toughest part, interviewing them. They're expecting you."

"What have you got, something from your scrapbook?"

Jim kept a file of newspaper clippings about cases out of our jurisdiction that held his interest, especially unsolved ones. This guy would have made a good MET officer. He was very thorough.

"Maybe nothing," said Jim. "I remembered a case last year in Needham, back in the fall, with a similar MO. A guy got his throat slit while sitting in his car in a parking lot late at night outside a restaurant where he worked. He was young, early twenties, Black, and the case was never solved, at least, not yet."

"They could be connected, but that would be a stretch. That was in the suburbs about ninety miles away, ten months ago." I knew better than to dismiss this, however.

"The similarities are striking, don't you think?"

"True. Do me a favor, will you, Jim? Look into that a little further. Make a call up to the Needham Police. See if they have anything new on it."

"No problem, Jack. Did you find those waitresses last night?"

I sipped more coffee and nodded slowly, my eyes straight ahead.

"I caught up with one of them, Millie Wallenski. She was devastated. Really took it hard. She had just left work before it happened and didn't know anything."

"You believe her story okay?"

"Yeah. Nobody can cry that hard while lying. I've got to find the other one, DeeDee O'Hare, today. She was out partying late after work, according to Millie Wallenski, so I'll ride over to her house again this morning. I hope she can give me something to work with. Then I'll see the Duartes."

"That was a heck of a knife job, Jack, wouldn't you say?"

I sipped coffee, looked down for a moment as if envisioning the crime scene again and then spoke. "The killer must have been waiting for the victim in the back seat of his car. Most young people on the Cape don't bother locking their cars. Safety's not on their radar. So the killer had no problem getting in. There's a chance the killer knew the victim, or at least knew the routine at the restaurant. Robbery wasn't the motive because they left behind a hundred in an envelope. The killer had to have a pretty good idea that the victim would be alone, you know, not likely to be giving anybody else a ride home after work."

"What about an employee," said Jim.

"The waitresses left before the victim and the Conleys were the only ones left," I said.

"So we need to find out more about the people who knew Manny Duarte besides those two waitresses. I guess you've got your work cut out, Detective."

"Well, I'll probably have to ask the Chief to assign me some help, so don't make any travel plans, Jimbo." I laughed. "Right now, I'll try to roust that other waitress."

"Good luck, Jack. I'll make that call to Needham for you."

I finished my coffee and checked my watch. It was almost ten thirty. Normally I would get an earlier start than this, but I knew a young partygoer was likely to be sleeping in, so there was no point in going earlier. But now, sleeping or not, DeeDee O'Hare was going to get a caller.

Chapter Five

Wearing brown slacks, green sport coat, yellow shirt and dark tie, I looked suitably *establishment* as I drove my police car along Route 28 to Depot Street and headed south. Two right turns put me on Center Street, and I slowed down to look for house number 28. I found the white ranch house on the right side of the road with several cars parked outside, two in single file in the driveway and two on the shoulder. I pulled past the cars and parked on the shoulder ahead of them.

As I walked up to the house, I noticed a young man and woman watching me through the picture window in the living room. When I reached the door, the young man opened it and greeted me. "Can I help you?" he asked.

"I'm Detective Contino from the Dennis Police Department. I'm trying to find DeeDee O'Hare. I understand she lives here."

They were both barefoot: the dark haired woman in blue jean cutoffs and yellow halter top, the man in khaki cutoffs and a white T-shirt. She seemed nervous. He was calm and cool.

"What's this about?" asked the young man. "Is she in some sort of trouble?"

"No. There was an incident last night at the restaurant where she works. I need to talk to all the employees."

The young man stepped back into the house, holding the door for me as I entered the living room. My holstered weapon showed briefly under my sport coat. I was unconcerned that it was momentarily exposed. A little show of force could be a good thing at times.

"What kind of incident?" he asked.

I paused for a moment, deciding whether or not to tell them. Then I let it out. "There was a murder outside The Beachgoer."

"Oh, my God," said the woman. She moved closer to the young man and grabbed his right arm.

I took out a small pad and pen from my coat pocket. "I'll need your names, please."

"I'm Judy Black," said the woman. "This is Scott Seldon."

I wrote down their names as they spoke and then looked at Judy. "Could you please get Miss O'Hare for me?"

Judy was about to move when a tall, slender young man with brownish hair emerged from a side hallway wearing jeans only. "What's going on?" he asked as he got closer to the group.

"Oh Jared, it's awful," said Judy. "There was a murder at The Beachgoer last night. This is Detective Contino with the police."

Summer on the Cape. Young people, twenty-somethings, single and with raging hormones. *There was a time,* I thought. I got the picture. Still, I had to ask. "Do you all live here?"

"Actually," said Judy with no hint of embarrassment, "DeeDee and I rent this house. Scott and Jared are our . . . friends. We met this summer and we're together a lot."

"That's right," said Jared. "I'm Jared Wilkes. I tend bar at the Chicken Roost and have a room there."

"I live in Boston and come down on the weekends," said Scott. "We met through mutual friends."

"Thank you all. Now if someone could please get Miss O'Hare for me."

Judy looked at Jared and her leg began to move reflexively. Jared cut her off, however, before she could take a step."

"I'll get her. Please give her a minute. She partied hard last night."

I nodded.

While Jared went back to the bedroom for DeeDee, the others stood in an awkward silence. Finally, Judy broke it. "Would you like a cup of coffee, Detective?"

"No, thank you."

"Say, ah, who was murdered?" asked Scott.

"His name was Manny Duarte, the bartender."

Judy gasped, looked at Scott and her eyes began to tear up. She tugged harder on Scott's arm. She turned toward him, burying her face in his shoulder. He closed his free arm around her.

"How well did you know him, Miss Black?"

Judy looked back at me. "Not real well, but he was a good guy. Sometimes, he'd join us at the beach on his day off, Monday. The restaurant is closed on Mondays." She looked at Scott.

"I'm back in Boston on Mondays so those were beach parties I missed," he said.

Jared returned alone to the group. "She'll be right out. She just needs some quick spiffing up. There's a bit of the Irish Pub still in her trying to pick a fight, but she's okay."

I heard footsteps and the sound of a door closing, probably the bathroom, then water running and a toilet flushing.

"What exactly happened, Detective?" asked Jared.

"Let me wait for Miss O'Hare and then you can all hear me at once, okay?"

"Yeah, sure," said Jared.

"Why don't we all sit down?" asked Judy. She and Scott took seats on the sofa along the inside wall of the living room.

I remained standing. Jared walked over to the front window and stared out at nothing in particular. DeeDee finally appeared from the bathroom wearing a long blue robe. She was barefoot like her friends and her blonde hair showed an attempt at combing. Not enough time for spiffy.

After introducing myself to DeeDee O'Hare, I motioned to the two chairs flanking the fireplace hearth. "Why don't you take a seat, Miss O'Hare?"

DeeDee sat down in the chair nearest the sofa and I took the other. Judy slid across the sofa from the middle section to the arm near DeeDee. Scott stayed at the other end. Jared was still looking out the window.

I told her about Manny Duarte and I got the expected response. Although she didn't break into tears like Millie Wallenski, there was a sufficient amount of shock. She didn't speak at first, as if her mouth suddenly went completely dry and she needed a saliva refill. Of course, she still had some cotton mouth from the night before, even after a quick but audible gargle during her visit to the bathroom.

She looked at Judy with an open mouth and they reached out hands to each other.

"How could this happen?" asked DeeDee. "When? We were just with him at work."

I gave them the facts about Manny's throat being cut while in his car and the Conley boy finding him shortly after closing time.

"Judy, would you please get me a glass of water?" asked DeeDee.

Judy jumped up without answering and fetched as requested. DeeDee took a fast drink when she had firmly wrapped both hands around the glass that her friend gave her.

"Miss O'Hare, did you see anything or anyone in the parking lot when you left work?"

"No, not that I recall."

"What do you recall, exactly, Miss O'Hare?"

"Well, I turned in my order pad and took my purse off the hook in the kitchen and left the building. I was in a hurry to leave, you know, Friday night and our friends were going to meet at the Irish." She glanced at Scott and Judy.

"On the way to your car, Miss O'Hare, you saw nothing unusual?"

"No sir. I knew Millie was close behind me, but that's all."

"What about bus boys?"

"Oh, we bus our own tables and Billy helps out. It keeps us busy, but Mr. Conley keeps his overhead low that way."

"Miss O'Hare, did you know if Manny had any enemies?"

"I really didn't know him outside of work."

"But you did see him at the beach sometimes, in a social context."

"Yes, a couple of times. But, other than that, I didn't talk to him much." She folded her arms and scratched at the side of her neck.

"Ever hear him say anything about drugs?"

"No, no, never."

"He took courses at the community college. Did he ever talk about people over there, friends, teachers, anybody?"

24

I paused. This was getting me nowhere. Maybe they weren't in a talking mood, or they just didn't know much about the guy.

"What's going to happen today?" DeeDee asked, as she looked around at her friends.

"The restaurant will be closed for a couple of days. I'm sure Mr. Conley will get in touch with you about when to report back to work."

Jared turned back toward the group and was looking at DeeDee, his arms folded across his chest.

I stood up. "Thanks for your help, Miss O'Hare." I took a card from my coat pocket and handed it to DeeDee. "If you think of anything else later, feel free to call me any time."

"Oh, sure."

I thanked the others and walked myself out. The others all stayed where they were. I put my notepad and pen away as I walked. Once in my car, I started the engine and let it idle for a moment as I took stock of the brief interview. The women seemed to know the victim, but there wasn't much reaction from the guys. DeeDee's boyfriend stayed well away from her during the whole thing. No effort at comforting her. That seemed unusual. Or maybe he's cop shy for some other reason. And the other guy on the sofa didn't stay close to his girlfriend when she moved closer to DeeDee. It might all mean nothing. It doesn't take much to put a chill on a summer romance. Murder can be a real turn off.

My next call wouldn't hold much fun, either.

Chapter Six

I hate doing this part.

My next stop was to call on Manny Duarte's family in Hyannis. It went as I expected. Funny, I felt that Jim Pearson had the tougher job last night, breaking the horrible news to the parents. I'm sure he was glad to have that over with and the follow-up was for me. Either way, it stinks.

Manny's dad, Andrew, worked on the maintenance staff at Cape Cod Hospital. His mom was a checkout clerk at Kmart. Manny had no enemies that they knew of and he didn't mess with drugs. His room had some sports memorabilia; a high school soccer team picture, a poster of Jim Rice of the Red Sox and a softball and glove on his dresser. He had a stereo in his room and a modest record collection: the Beatles, Neil Diamond, Chuck Berry and other artists I didn't know.

He had a younger brother, Michael, who politely greeted me when I said hello to him and then didn't speak again during my visit. I assured the Duartes that I would do my best to find Manny's killer, left my card with them and drove away. If they had any pertinent information to help in my investigation, I didn't get it today.

I drove back to the office and caught Jim Pearson as he was leaving. He was about to get into his car when he saw me approaching, so he stood next to his door waiting for me to pull up. I stopped next to him and got out of my cruiser.

"I called the Needham PD, Jack. I spoke to the Deputy Chief. He said he'd be happy to cooperate since the two murders had similarities. But he didn't have anything off hand that he could offer. He'll look into the case and get back to you. I gave him your name and phone."

"Thanks, Jimbo. Now get out of here. Don't you know it's Saturday?"

"Guess I'm not the only one around here with a defective calendar." Jim entered his car and left.

I had no personal connections on the Needham PD so I decided to enlist some other help. My old partner on the Metropolitan District Commission Police, Leo Barbado, wasn't happy when I announced my retirement and my intention to move to Cape Cod. We had been together a long time and busted many bad guys along the way. Leo retired from the METs shortly after I did and started his own private detective business, Barbado Investigations. We kept in close touch.

He answered the phone after three rings.

"Leo, I need you to check into an old case for me."

"I'm fine and so's the wife and kids. Thanks for asking. And how's everything with you, Beachbum?"

"I don't have time for phone etiquette, pal. I've got a nasty-looking murder down here. It looks something like a case in Needham last fall, so I need to look for a possible connection. What wife and kids?"

"Just yanking your chain. What's the local PD got for you?"

"Nothing yet, and I don't know how long it might take for them to dig anything up, so I thought I'd hire a dirt digger, just to give me an edge."

"Was that hire, as in work for money?"

"Money? What's that? I'll treat you to an all-expenses paid weekend at Casa Contino on the Cape."

"Does the room come with bourbon, beer and dancing girls?"

"Two out of three, buddy boy. You can guess which two."

"What about chow?"

"Meals included, all you can eat."

"As long as you don't do the cooking, you're on."

I told Leo about the Manny Duarte murder and the information Jim Pearson found out about the Needham case. He agreed to sniff around for a connection, but didn't think he'd find one. Sniffing and dirt digging were two things Leo was very good at doing. I felt better already, but not by much.

I started running checks with the local police departments, State Police, Boston PD and the FBI on all the kids

I'd met so far in the investigation. It was just routine stuff and I didn't expect it to turn up anything, but you never know. They all seemed like typical twenty-somethings, but looks can be deceiving. I had a slightly negative feeling about Jared Wilkes. There was nothing concrete about it. He just rubbed me the wrong way for some reason.

The circle around this crime was small. Unless Manny was involved with something or somebody we hadn't turned up yet, there weren't many potential actors in this play. I might have already talked to the killer.

Chapter Seven

Jared was dressing when Will stopped in the open doorway to Jared's room above the Chicken Roost. He folded his arms across his chest, sleeves rolled up to his elbows and leaned one shoulder against the door frame.

"Nice suit," he said as Jared stood inside the room, his back to Will, combing his full head of evenly-cut, long, dark hair.

The suit was Mod style, cut very trim, which fitted Jared's tall, lean frame perfectly. Charcoal with a four button jacket that buttoned high toward the neck, it showed little of the white shirt and blue tie. The lapels were slim and the three button cuff had a velvet tab that matched the velvet collar. It had a flap collar on the left breast. The boots were jet black with a spit shine and thick heels. Jared turned around and stood straight before Will, as if modeling his outfit.

"Very impressive, Jared."

"Glad you like it, Will. I got this a couple of years ago when I went to England. If you ever want to borrow it, feel free."

Will laughed, with a bit of smoker's cough rumbling through it. "Hah! I think the waist would fit, but you're a little taller than me. Besides, I think May would say it's not my style. I'm thirty some years too old for that one."

"I'll be back in plenty of time for my shift."

Will looked down as he spoke. "It was a terrible thing that happened. I hope the Conleys will be all right, not to mention the kid's family. They must be really shook."

Jared made no comment as he stepped past Will and walked slowly down the back stairs. He went into the cocktail lounge and peered out the front window. He was expecting DeeDee to pick him up.

Jared drove a 1969 Opel Kadett, a small German-made car sold by General Motors in America. It worked, but made many unappreciated noises that didn't inspire confidence in the driver. He didn't like to be seen in it very often. DeeDee had a 1973 Dodge Dart, light green with lots of shiny chrome, so Jared talked DeeDee into driving her car when they were together, provided her sobriety level was sufficient. He'd take the wheel when she arrived.

Jared stood looking out the window, his hands folded in front of him, his eyes closed for brief periods, almost like he was meditating. Within two minutes he heard the sound of the Dart pulling into the parking lot. He opened his eyes, confirmed that it was DeeDee and left the building through the front door.

Jared looked at the Dodge Dart, his eyes traveling along its side as he walked to the driver's side door. DeeDee slid awkwardly across the console separating the front bucket seats and settled into the passenger side. She looked at Jared and he returned her glance. Neither of them spoke. Funerals don't make for much happy talk.

Chapter Eight

The service started at ten o'clock and lasted about forty-five minutes. I took a place in the last pew in the section to the left of the aisle. Jared and DeeDee were in the rear pew on the right side, but they didn't notice me. Millie Wallenski came in alone and went through a side aisle to move in beside DeeDee. The Conleys were in the third row from the front. The Duarte family and close friends occupied the first two rows of the left section. At the conclusion of the service, the family members proceeded down the center aisle slowly, some weeping. I noticed a tall, young Black man among the Duarte family members staring across the aisle at DeeDee. She seemed to make eye contact with him and quickly looked away.

The funeral procession went to a small cemetery in South Dennis. The air was warm, but there was a sea breeze keeping the people relatively cool. It was six days since Manny's murder. The shock had worn off most except the family, many of whom wept openly at the grave side. The Conleys had reopened the Beachgoer on Tuesday, with DeeDee and Millie resuming their work schedules. One more day and another weekend would start, another time for the weekenders to cross the bridges onto the Cape to spend their money, another time for the young people to arrive to meet up with their summer resident friends and to satisfy their hormonal urges.

I stood a respectful distance away from the crowd at the funeral, watching as the people I had interviewed paid their respects. Scott Seldon was not present, but since he was a weekender I didn't expect to see him. The Conley family, Millie Wallenski, and DeeDee O'Hare showed faces typical of people who had been moved by a sudden death in their lives. I couldn't help notice that Jared Wilkes was an exception. He stood straight and without emotion the entire time. Maybe that was just his way.

I watched Jared look down at DeeDee and nod agreement to whatever she was saying. They turned from the crowd and moved away quietly. DeeDee squeezed Millie's arm as they departed, and Millie returned the gesture by tapping DeeDee's hand. Jared caught sight of me in the distance. My eyes locked onto Jared's for a brief, cold moment.

Chapter Nine

There was something about this Wilkes character that was getting under my skin. Maybe it was just his cool manner. But maybe it was too cool. He didn't seem at all shaken by Manny's murder. I needed to know more about him.

The day after the funeral, I stopped by the Chicken Roost to speak with Wilkes. It was about three o'clock in the afternoon, and an older gent was behind the bar. It was a cheaply made bar, pine wood planks, heavily varnished. The guy probably had limited cash. Not a bad job, considering.

"Excuse me. I'm Detective Jack Contino, Dennis Police. I'd like to speak with Jared Wilkes."

"Not here right now. He comes on at four. I'm Will Souther, owner. Can I help you?" The man's voice was low and gravelly, like a lot of men who had a long history of chain smoking. But I didn't see any cigarettes burning. He must have kicked the habit.

"Hello, Mr. Souther."

"Just Will. No need to get formal, Detective."

"Okay, Will. I'm investigating the murder of Manny Duarte."

"Glad to help out, but I don't know what I can offer you. That sure was a terrible thing."

"Was Jared working here that night?"

"Yep. I was helping May in the kitchen, and Jared tended the bar."

"What time did he get off duty?"

"Oh, I let him go just before midnight. One of his young friends met him here and they headed off to the Irish Pub to catch up with their crowd, so I told him to skedaddle. I closed up the bar. I hope you don't think Jared had anything to do with it, 'cause, like I say, he was right here."

"I just have to check out all avenues, that's all. What can you tell me about Jared?"

"Well, I just met him last winter. I was looking to hire a bartender and he applied for the job. May and me have had this place for ten years. We applied for a liquor license every year and last fall we finally got it. So I took out a loan, built this room as an addition to the place and set it up as the bar and lounge. Jared was a great help. I didn't know much about setting up a bar and he just took it over for me, knew exactly what to do, since he had bartending experience before at some other Cape establishments."

"Where did he work before coming here?"

"He ran the bar at the Hotel Belmont for a couple of years. That's a big place, so he didn't have any trouble setting up my little joint. And a few years back, he was a Boston firefighter." Will's posture straightened up when he said that, like a guy speaking proudly of his own son.

"Why'd he leave the BFD?"

"He took a bad fall from a ladder while out on a call during the winter. Broke his leg and it never really healed right. So, he got a disability, left the department and moved to the Cape. Been here ever since."

"That's very interesting. You wouldn't happen to have a copy of his resume, would you?"

Will let out a soft laugh. "Resume! Hah, the only resume I ask for is what a guy can tell me. Then if he shows me he can do the job, I hire him. Oh, I did call the Belmont and he checked out there. I can tell if a guy's not being straight up with me."

"Sounds like you have a lot of faith in Jared."

"Yep. He's top shelf. Hope he stays with us for a good long time. I even pay him a bonus now and then. Well, I don't exactly pay him. He sort of pays himself. All bartenders hit the till a bit. I know it and he knows I know it. But it's okay, 'cause he's worth it. I figure he brings in enough business with his buddies stopping by a lot. They spend some. He takes some."

I shook my head and grinned. "That sure is an interesting bonus system you have there, Will."

"Ah, it's okay. Like I said, he's worth it. Heck, maybe he'll marry that young honey of his and buy me out. May and me ain't getting any younger. We'd like to have a couple more good years here and then cash it in and go to Florida."

"Sounds like he'd be buying you out with your own money."

Will's face went serious and then broke into a grin. "More like his pals' money, but just the down payment."

"Well, I hope you get your wish. Thanks, Will. You have a great day, now."

Not likely, I thought. Wilkes didn't go with the phrase *great day.*

Chapter Ten

"I'm afraid somebody fed you a cock and bull story about Jared Wilkes."

I held the phone as close to my ear as I could without climbing into it. It was Ron Alberts, an old friend on the Boston Fire Department, returning a call I made after my talk with Will Souther. "Don't tell me he never worked on the BFD," I said.

"Oh, he worked here, all right. But he was no hero. He never broke his leg on the job and he's not collecting a disability from the City."

"For some reason, I'm not surprised, Ron. He doesn't strike me as the hero type. So why did he leave the FD?"

"He was asked to leave, well, not exactly asked. In 1971 the racial climate was pretty bad in the city. You know how it was."

"Yeah, those were tough years. I like to think it's getting better."

"Me too, Jack. Well, the BFD had its share of guys who weren't ready to ride alongside any Blacks. Jared Wilkes was one of them and he had a habit of making his feelings known out loud. He was disciplined twice for incidents he caused right in the firehouse. He tried to stir up trouble by getting some of his fellow racists to slash the tires on a Black firefighter's car. They even broke into it and defecated on the back seat. The two guys got thrown off the Department."

"I remember something about that, Ron, but I don't recall the name Wilkes."

"The two who got canned named Wilkes as the guy who put them up to it but it wasn't enough to throw him off, so he got away with a reprimand again. Me, I'd have said three strikes and you're out, but, hey, the powers that be saw it otherwise. Anyway, a couple months later, he got into a fight with the same Black guy right in the firehouse and that was it. The Black got a suspension and Wilkes got shown the door."

"Interesting that Wilkes got some other guys to do his dirty work."

"I don't know if this will help you, Jack."

"Well, it might. I sure know a lot more about Mr. Wilkes now and have definite reason to hate his guts. Thanks, Ron. I really appreciate this."

"Anytime, old buddy."

I hung up the phone and stroked my chin. I didn't have any real evidence for the case but at least I knew that Jared Wilkes was a liar who wasn't above getting other people to do his bidding.

Chapter Eleven

It was getting late in the day and I figured DeeDee O'Hare would be going to work soon at The Beachgoer. Ed Conley had hired a new bartender, probably a temp, so the place was opened for business again. I wanted to learn more about Jared Wilkes, and the gal who slept with him would be a good candidate for information. Pillow talk had a way of creeping into investigations before.

I pulled up to DeeDee's rental house, parked directly in front and went up to the door. Judy Black answered my knock and let me in. She was wearing a red bikini and must have just come in from a sun bathing session. She was shimmering with lotion and perspiration.

"Hello, Detective. Can I help you?"

"Yes. I'd like to see Miss O'Hare, please. Is she in?"

"She's getting ready for work. I'll get her."

Judy disappeared down the hall and in a few seconds DeeDee emerged in her waitress outfit.

"Hello. Detective Contino, was it?"

"That's correct. I need to speak with you for a few minutes."

"I have to go to work soon. I hope this won't take long," she said, fidgeting with her short, black skirt.

I heard a door close down the hall, followed by the sound of a shower running. I guessed it was Judy Black's turn.

I motioned for DeeDee to take a seat and she slowly lowered herself onto the sofa while I sat in a chair near her. I grabbed my notepad from a coat pocket and reviewed what little I had from our previous talk.

"How long have you known Jared Wilkes?"

"I met him earlier this summer. Didn't I mention that before?" Her brow wrinkled a bit.

"Did you know anything about him before that?"

"No, I didn't. Like I said, Detective, we just met."

"And you've had a close relationship with him these past couple of months?"

"Look, we're over twenty-one, Detective. We can do what we want. It's not against the law for us to sleep together, is it?" She folded her arms across her chest.

"No. Miss O'Hare, it's not. Has he ever told you about his background, in general, like some of his previous jobs?"

"Not much. He told me that he broke his leg once when he was a Boston fireman and he had to give that job up. He doesn't like to talk about it. And he's had other bartending jobs on the Cape. He's kind of a free spirit, you know. He likes to go his own way. He even went to live in England for a while when he was younger, just out of high school."

"How did that go for him?"

"He said it was a great time. I guess he liked the clothing styles there, you know, the Mod look. It's kind of the way the Beatles used to look when they first got famous. Say, why all these questions about Jared? You don't think he had anything to do with Manny's murder, do you? He couldn't have. He was working at the Chicken Roost. You must know that."

"Yes, Miss O'Hare, I do know that. I just need to round out the big picture here." I hoped that phrase was sufficiently vague to satisfy her. "How well did he know Manny?"

"Not very. He's been at the beach a couple of times with our group. Frankly, I don't think he particularly cared for Manny."

"Why do you suppose that was?"

"Well, Manny and I worked together, so we were friends. When we were at the beach, Manny would talk to me, clown around a bit and even sit next to me. One time when Manny was beside me on a blanket, Jared came over and took my hand, pulled me up to my feet and said we needed to go for a walk. Maybe he was a little jealous. I don't know, but he was just cold toward Manny."

"Did they ever argue or fight?"

"No, no, Detective. Nothing like that. Jared is good and kind. He'd never hurt anyone. And he's very generous. He always tips fellow bartenders very well."

"Yes, I understand how that goes. So, he gets along fine with everybody else in your group?"

"Of course, Detective."

"Does he have any hobbies, interests, or so forth, when not working?"

"Besides me?" She broke into a smile for the first time. "He likes to listen to music, some Caribbean style, like Calypso. It's pretty cool. Look, Detective, I've got to get to work. Is there anything else?"

"Not right now, Miss O'Hare. Thank you for your time. Remember, you can call me any time."

"Why would I want to do that? I don't know what else there is to tell you."

"Well, just to let you know that you can, that's all. Would you tell Miss Black that I'd like to talk to her, too, as soon as she's ready?"

"Sure. I've got to go now."

I wasn't surprised to hear that Wilkes was cold toward Manny. If Manny seemed to be flirting with DeeDee, that could make a guy jealous, and jealousy could lead to rage. But I wondered if there was something more.

I sat on the living room sofa and waited for Judy Black. After several minutes, she emerged from the bathroom with a towel around her and another in her hands. She rubbed her hair with it.

"I guess it's my turn," she said. She stopped rubbing her hair and took a seat in a chair to my left. The towel around her rode up as she sat and crossed her legs, but I managed to keep my eyes trained on her face. This wasn't going to be easy.

"Tell me, Miss Black, was there any friction between Jared Wilkes and Manny Duarte? I ask because Miss O'Hare said there was an incident at the beach recently where Wilkes was cold toward Manny, even rude."

"Oh, I know what she was talking about. There was this one day where a bunch of us were at the beach. Let's see, there was me, DeeDee, Jared, Manny, Millie and her friend, Fran. At one point, Jared told Manny to get him a beer from the cooler. He said come on, hop to it. You're a bartender. Don't make a Federal case out of it."

"What happened next?"

"So Manny opened the cooler and fetched a beer from it. He held it toward Jared, but Jared didn't take it. Instead, he looked at Manny kind of funny, almost mad. Manny

40

stared back at Jared, but he got the message. He had to open it and then give it to Jared. Jared took it and walked away from the group, pulling DeeDee by the hand with him. She looked back at Manny almost apologizing."

"So Wilkes was very condescending to Duarte."

"Yes, he was. I told Manny not to worry about it, that Jared was really a good guy. He said something like *yeah, he's a real peach.* He said if a shark bit Jared it might get food poisoning."

"Did Manny ever come on strong to DeeDee, or was that only in Jared's mind?"

"Well, I know he looked at DeeDee a lot at the beach. Why not? She's got a great body, so of course he looked. He's a guy. Well, I told Manny I was glad he finally joined us for a beach day. He said he had other stuff to do most of the time, but on that day he thought, what the hell, why not. I asked him for a beer and he got me one and he told me not to get plastered. I guess he was flirting with me, since DeeDee was off with Jared. That was okay with me, since Manny had a pretty good body himself, tall, dark and athletic. He looked great in a tight bathing suit."

"Did anything else happen at the beach?"

"Not much. I told Manny I needed some more suntan lotion on my back and he offered to do the honors. That was, well, nice of him."

"I'm sure he struggled through the task."

Judy smiled at me when I said that. *I wish I hadn't.*

"So he just squirted a stream of lotion from the bottle and rubbed it on my back and legs. He got a little fresh when his hands ran up my sides, you know, letting his fingertips just nudge my breasts. It was okay, though. He really didn't step over the line. I could hear Millie and her friend giggling."

I bet Miss Black allowed a very wide line for guys to cross. I would have enjoyed hearing Duarte's version of that day at the beach.

It was time to end this interview, so I got up, thanked Miss Black for her time and made a straight line for the front door. I wondered if Nat would like to go to the beach on the weekend.

Chapter Twelve

Leo Barbado felt like he was working with his old partner again, even if the partner was an hour and a half away in Dennis.

The Needham PD hadn't come up with anything on that ten-month-old murder. Okay. They had limited resources, but the State Police should have found something by now. The whole thing was too quiet. Leo decided to call in a favor.

It was a warm summer day just past morning rush hour and Leo was glad he finally owned a car with air conditioning. He had enough self-denial in his life. He wasn't getting any younger, and it was time for a little self-indulgence. What an extravagance. It helped make the trip to the Framingham barracks much easier.

Leo went through the usual security stops, identified himself and parked in the visitor's section of the front parking lot. He approached the front desk in the lobby and spoke to the desk sergeant, an old acquaintance. "Hello, Sergeant Leary. I'm here to see Major Hawkins."

"Nice to see you, Detective. You know, you could pass for Dean Martin's younger brother, six feet, nice build, and enough wavy dark hair to make me jealous. You and Jack Contino haven't been around for a while. I heard he's retired."

"Yes, and it's Mr. Barbado. I'm not representing the METs anymore, either. I retired awhile back and started my own business, Barbado Investigations."

"That sounds cool. So what's Jack Contino doing? He working with you?"

"He's down the Cape working on his tan and some of us still have to work for a living."

"Funny you should mention that. I retire, myself, in a week, but I need to find some work to supplement my pension. I got a kid at Dartmouth and another one looking at Mt. Holyoke next year. I'm going to need a little extra cash flow myself. You wouldn't happen to need a big, tough, smart, compassionate, hardworking, extremely talented law enforcement officer, would you?"

"You need to check with our personnel department."

"You're kidding. You've got a Personnel Department?"

"Of course. You're looking at it." Leo took out his wallet, extracted a business card and handed it to the sergeant. "Send me your resume. No offense, but we have to have one on file for all our people, just in case some pain-in-the-ass lawyer wants to insinuate in court that an investigator is unqualified."

"I understand. No offense taken."

"I call in help as we need it."

"Do you need it now?"

"With Tommy Shea and the Winter Hill boys still breaking the laws of the land, I'm sure I can find some work for you. It's not always exciting. May only be part time, mind you. There's a lot of trying to track down missing persons. Of course, Shea and his pals often cause people to go missing. Sometimes it's just pissed off girlfriends trying to get away from abusive boyfriends or teenage runaways. I'm sure I can help you put your kids through college. I don't envy you."

"No kids?"

"Nope. No wife. It's simpler that way."

"I can only imagine. You didn't hear that, Mr. Barbado."

"Hear what?"

The sergeant smiled and put Leo's card in his shirt pocket. He rang for Major Hawkins. In a minute or so, Clint Hawkins came into the lobby, greeted Leo and escorted him down the hall and into his office.

"Good to see you again, Leo. You haven't given us the pleasure of your company for some time now."

"Well, I save my visits for special occasions; holidays, birthdays, homicides." Leo took a seat in front of Clint's desk while Hawkins put his tall, powerfully-built body into his high back leather chair.

"Something new I should know about?"

"Something old I need some information about. A young Black guy got his throat cut in Needham last fall. The Needham PD says the victim is clean, as far as they can tell. He doesn't have a record, doesn't show up on any databases, and they don't have any leads. Seems strange to me they're still dry after all this time. Have you got anything on it?"

Major Hawkins sat with his hands folded on his desk, like he was posing for an official photograph. He took a long, labored breath after Leo spoke, looked down at his hands and then looked at Leo. "I do remember that case, Leo. I'm very familiar with it."

"Very familiar," said Leo. "Not just familiar, that's significant."

"Leo, old friend, I'm afraid that I'm not at liberty to discuss the details of that case at this time. I hope you understand."

"Not at liberty to discuss?" Leo looked straight at Clint Hawkins for a few silent seconds and Hawkins returned the look, as if the photo shoot wasn't over. "I get it. This case is a much bigger deal than it appears to be on the surface. Big enough so that even the local PD gets the silent treatment?"

Hawkins nodded very slowly. "I can't tell you that. Like I said, I'm not at liberty to discuss the details."

Leo understood. "Well, thanks for not telling me that. Needham's a clean little town. They don't have homicides too often. We have a lot of them connected to Somerville due to the Winter Hill boys. What's Needham got, the Bird's Hill boys?"

"Bird's Hill?"

"It's a section of town with a train station there. Don't you ever ride the train?"

"No, Leo, I stick to my cruiser."

"If it's too big a case to let the Needham PD in on the details, can I assume that the Feds *are* in on it?"

Hawkins nodded in the same way again.

"Thanks for not telling me that, too. I guess you haven't told me about as much as I can expect." Leo rose up from his chair.

"You haven't told me why you're so interested in this case, Leo."

"There was a murder on the Cape recently with a similar M.O. It happened in Jack Contino's town. One of his guys remembered the Needham murder. Jack checked it out for a possible connection, but when the Needham PD couldn't give him much, he asked me to sniff around."

"So Jack's still working?"

"Oh, yeah, Chief of Detectives on the Dennis PD. You can't keep a good man down."

"Not that man. I'm not surprised he couldn't just hang up the badge and go fishing."

"It's been nice chatting with you, Clint, very non-informative."

"Same here, Leo. And Leo, I say this as an old friend. Be careful sniffing around this one."

Chapter Thirteen

I was stirring my coffee in a Styrofoam cup while sitting at my office desk when the phone rang. It was just after 11:00 in the morning.

"Want to hear a riddle?" the voice asked.

"Good morning, Leo."

"What do you call a cold case, ten months old, your good friends at the State Police won't talk about it and the local PD is in the dark?"

I took a minute before answering. I sipped some of my coffee. "A Federal case."

"You win the big prize, Jacko, a no-expense paid trip to Boston and a tour of the Boston FBI-HQ. When do you want to come up?"

"Hold on a minute, Leo. Slow down. You're telling me you got shut out by the Staties?"

"That's right. I dropped by to talk with Clint Hawkins. He said he was not at liberty to discuss details of the case. He was as informative as he could be in, shall we say, a non-verbal kind of way."

"Yeah, sometimes it's what somebody doesn't say."

"Exactly. And we know that when the State Police are mum and are keeping the locals in the dark, there's probably a Federal presence lurking."

"Which means that either the victim, Mr. Cleanjeans, isn't so clean or there are other characters in this play who we don't know about yet." I sipped some more coffee, taking in too much. It burned a bit going down. "So if Hawkins won't, or can't, talk then maybe we go over his head."

"Good old Agent Nelson."

"The one and only. Haven't seen him in quite awhile. I'll pick you up at your place around one. We can grab a bite and then head to town. Call Nelson, will you? Let him know we're coming over."

"Will do, pal. See you in a few."

I really didn't enjoy driving into Boston anymore. It was part of my past and I guess I was feeling older. I used to have no problem traipsing about the city going after bad guys. Now, I could pass it up, but the job said otherwise. Well, I hadn't been to the Government Center in a long time.

I told my Chief where I was going and why and then called Natalie at home to give her the news, just in case. I took a Dennis PD squad car, figuring that it could help if I hit tight traffic, and headed for the Mid-Cape Highway. Even when you're out of jurisdiction, it can be to your advantage to have the lights, a siren and the word *Police* written across the car. It was an overcast day, which made the drive a little easier for me. I don't like the hard glare of the sun.

It was near one o'clock when I pulled up to Leo's place. I knew he was watching for me from his office window, so I just pulled up alongside a parked car at the curb and waited, not turning off the engine. He didn't take long. After our usual greetings, "Hi ya, Beachbum," "Up yours, Dipstick," we stopped at a local sub shop, got two Italian cold cut subs, wolfed them down with sodas and left for Boston.

The Government Center Plaza was only about a decade and a-half old, with a handful of new office buildings. The City Hall building is the most eye catching part of the eight acre area, broader at the top than at the bottom and looking like a series of cantilevered concrete structures overlooking a brick courtyard. Some people love it. Some hate it. The FBI offices were in the JFK Building nearby. I identified myself to the lot attendant outside the underground garage and he checked his list of expected visitors.

"You guys are okay. Just put this on your dash."

He handed me a parking permit. I gave the permit to Leo, who did as instructed. I backed the squad car into an open space near the end of the first level. It's an old habit of mine. Those spin out turns in reverse are strictly for movie stuntmen. If I have to pull out quickly, I want to see where the hell I'm going.

It was a warm day, but not too hot, thanks to the clouds. We took our sport coats out of the back seat, slipped into them almost simultaneously and walked out of the garage and over to the complex known as the John F. Ken-

47

nedy Building. It is actually three buildings connected by enclosed walkways. The FBI headquarters took us up one of the two towers next to a four story low rise. Agent Nelson was waiting for us in his office on the ninth floor. Once inside, we exchanged short greetings.

"Nice to see you again, Jack," he said. "Hello, Leo."

"Likewise," I said.

Leo shrugged.

"What can I do for you, Jack?" Agent Nelson turned as he spoke and walked behind his desk, pulled his chair out a bit and eased into it. Leo and I sat across the desk in padded wooden chairs.

"A man was murdered in Needham last October and the local PD can't get anything to go on. It's going cold on them."

Agent Nelson sat with his arms folded across each other on his desk. He said nothing.

"Leo tried to talk to Clint Hawkins, State PD, and got the silent treatment."

"Leo?"

"He's working as a consultant for me in his spare time."

"Oh, you're a PI now, Barbado?"

"Right," said Leo.

That clarified that. Maybe.

"Help me out here, Jack. You're with the Dennis PD and you're looking into a ten month old murder in Needham?"

"A young Black man was murdered in Dennis a couple of weeks ago, very similar. It was outside a restaurant as the place was closing. Guy's throat was slit. The weapon's nowhere to be found and nobody saw anything."

Agent Nelson never flinched when I mentioned the Needham murder, but he raised an eyebrow just a twitch when I told him about the one at the Beachgoer.

"What makes you think I can help you, Jack?"

"Come on, Agent Nelson. Leo and I have been at this game too long. And remember, we used to play on your team a lot. We know how to read the signs."

It was Leo's time to chime in. "Clint Hawkins is a good man, Agent, and he kept quiet. But it doesn't take a genius to figure out that he had orders to keep quiet."

"So you think there's a Federal case here?"

"You tell me," I said. "Look, we did a lot of work for you over the years. We're not just a couple of local yokels. Don't close us out here. Maybe we can help each other again."

Agent Nelson looked down at his desk for a moment and then gazed at me, then Leo. He scratched his chin.

"I know about the Needham case, but your Dennis murder is a surprise. You think there is a connection?"

"Seems likely," I said. "Coincidences like that are kinda rare, don't you think?"

Agent Nelson leaned forward a bit at his desk, as if he was about to tell us a big bad secret. "There was more to that Needham killing than the Needham PD needs to know. No need to have too many partners. The victim was talking to us about a guy who was extorting him."

"Money," I said.

"No, more than that. The kid had been borrowing money to bet with and he was a loser. The debt got big and the shark turned out to be somebody in the Mob. He started forcing the kid to do odd jobs, illegal odd jobs, of course. We decided to plant an undercover agent at the place where he worked to learn as much as possible. Sometimes the loan shark made contact with him there. We wanted to get the shark, but we also wanted his boss and maybe close the whole operation. You've worked with the agent before. She's Tammy Watson. She was . . ."

"Oh, Jesus, no!" I said. Leo looked up as if he was about to pray. "I thought you sent her back to D.C. under cover? I'll say she worked under the covers."

"Jack, you don't know that. She never compromised herself."

"Oh, no. She just slept with Sammy White and you do know who he is."

"Jack, she always called in from her own place. Her phone records bear that out."

"Yeah, she called in dutifully at about five in the morning each time. Gave her plenty of time to give White what he wanted."

"Jack."

Tammy Watson was not my idea of a great FBI agent. Like me, she grew up in Somerville and she was in school with Tommy Shea, a young man who had been on my enemies list for years. They were a few years younger than

49

me, so we never crossed paths in school, but Shea became a problem kid who had many confrontations with the law. He spent some time in juvie. He and I once jammed outside a bar and he cut me with a shard of bottle glass. I slapped around pretty good and won the battle. But the war was going to be long term.

Because of her Somerville connection, the Bureau thought she'd work well under cover while trying to break up the Mob in Somerville. She got cozy with Shea's right hand man, Salvatore DiFino, aka Sammy White, and gave him a perfect alibi in the case of a Mob massacre one night in the North End a few years ago. She was keeping his feet warm and his toes curled that night.

I thought that she had been sent back to Washington, D.C., but I was wrong. So here she was again in Boston screwing things up. No pun intended.

"Well, so what happened? If she was right there at the restaurant, how'd they get to, what's his name, Allenson?"

"Allenson wasn't the target."

"What?" I asked.

"He was an innocent bystander. We think the hit man made a mistake. Got the wrong guy."

"So where's the real target?"

"I can't tell you that, just that he's under protection. He left work early that night and Agent Watson had no reason to expect anything was going to happen. They bungled the hit."

Leo looked at me incredulous. "Jack, those guys don't bungle hits. Sammy White would have cut the guy up into little pieces and stuffed 'em in a pizza box."

"So what happened?" I asked.

Agent Nelson shook his head. "Don't know. But Agent Watson's still working on it."

"I'll bet she is," said Leo. "And taking her sweet time about it."

"Look," said Agent Nelson. "That's all I can tell you about the case right now, but this similar killing in Dennis might be connected in some way to the one in Needham. Here's what we can do. If you and Leo can dig into the Dennis case, using your, ah, years of experience and talent in such matters, look for anything that might connect the murders. Let me know what you've got."

50

"Gee," I said. "That sounds like a one-way street to me. My idea of working together means I know *everything,* Agent Nelson. It's hard to operate in the dark." I stared at Agent Nelson with my best *this really pisses me off* look.

"I can't do that now, Jack." He sat back in his chair, content that he was one up on me. "You'll just have to trust me. If you come up with a connection, then I'll be able to give you more."

Leo looked at me. "That's all, Jack. We just have to come up with a connection, maybe even solve the case, maybe both of them. Nothing to it."

I wiped my hand over my face. "Agent, you have to let me talk to anybody and I mean *anybody* I deem necessary. If I have to operate in the dark, at least let me light a match."

"Yeah, sure, but don't tell the Needham PD what you know. I'll brief Hawkins at the State Police about today's meeting."

"I want to start with Agent Watson," I said.

"Now, Jack . . ."

"You agreed I could talk to anybody, so I start with her. How do I get in touch with her?"

"You don't. I'll call her in. It's a little past two. Go get some lunch and I'll have her here by two forty-five."

Leo spoke. "No can do. I have to watch my figure. We ate lunch already."

"So go get a cup of coffee or take a nap. I don't care. Be back here at two forty-five."

We found our way to the cafeteria on the ground floor, bought some coffee and grabbed a table near a window looking out on the courtyard. It was nearly one-thirty, but a number of people were still buying lunch. I spotted a tall guy with a familiar face in the checkout line. "Hey, isn't that Tom . . . ?"

"Yeah, that's him, from WBZ. He does some of their training programs on videotape. It's like a real TV station. I got to see it once last year."

"Amazing," I said. "The FBI goes showbiz. J. Edgar would have loved that."

We drank our coffee slowly, and I kept checking my watch. Bad idea. Time seemed to crawl by. Maybe there was a tour group we could join. Or a gift shop. Anything. After eternity came and went, we headed back to Agent Nelson's office.

Tammy Watson was already there when we went in, seated in the chair I had used earlier. A third chair had been pulled into place. Agent Nelson was still behind his desk as Leo and I sat down.

"Let's get to it," said Agent Nelson.

No introductions needed. No wisecracks from me or Leo. Agent Nelson was exercising control over this meeting. Good for him.

"There's been a murder in my jurisdiction that's similar to the one in Needham where you were under cover," I said.

"I know. I've just been briefed," said Agent Watson.

She was still a good-looking woman, pushing fifty, with long dark hair. Even sitting, I could tell she cut a good figure in her tight jeans and pink sleeveless top. Her arms showed just the right amount of muscle for a woman. At least she took her workouts seriously, if not her police work.

"Are you still in touch with Sammy White?"

"Sure, he's still my prime contact."

"Seems you're taking your time getting something on him," said Leo.

"Hey, you should try this job sometime. Some cops stay undercover with the Mob for years. It's not easy work, Barbado, and your neck is always out there."

"Sure it's not just your neck you're putting out?" said Leo.

"You always were a wise ass, Barbado."

"How about sticking to business," said Agent Nelson. "I don't want this to go on into the night."

I didn't mind Leo's barb, but I agreed with Agent Nelson. *Let's get this over with.* I couldn't stand being in the same room with her. "Has White, or any of your contacts, ever said anything about any jobs on the Cape?"

"No, nothing."

"Well, if they ever do, I need to hear about it right away. There's got to be a connection between these cases."

"Hey, Jack, your thing could be totally separate. Somebody could have read about it in the newspaper and remembered it when they got pissed off at some poor slob."

"The poor slob had a name, Manny Duarte."

"Whatever, Jack. I'm just saying, don't assume there's a link, 'cause there probably isn't. Manny Duarte, huh? I'll keep listening for any mention of him. Got anything else about him I should know?"

"No, just that he tended bar at a place called the Beach-goer in Dennis. He hung out with a summer crowd, some kids named DeeDee O'Hare, Jared Wilkes, Judy Black, Millie Wallenski." Watson stared at me as if to say "You expect me to remember all that?" so I wrote the names down for her on a slip of paper and handed it to her. She took it and folded it once, keeping it in her fingers.

"Anything else, Jack?" said Agent Nelson.

I looked at Leo, then turned back to Agent Watson. "No, not right now."

She was on her feet in an instant, looking at Agent Nelson. "Okay, that's it, Agent Watson. You can go." She gave me and Leo a look and then left.

Leo and I nodded in unison and pushed up out of our chairs. "Thanks for your help, Agent Nelson. We'll keep in touch." We started to leave and I stopped and turned back to him. I took a card out of my wallet and handed it to him. "My new home."

"Thanks, Jack. Good luck on your case."

While heading back to the garage, Leo spoke without looking at me. "Sure was a pleasure seeing Agent Watson again. Someday we're going to nail her ass, too, in a law enforcement way, I mean."

"I know what you mean, Leo, and I can't wait for that day to come. I think we'd better keep an eye on her, too."

"How're we going to do that? She knows us."

"I don't know. Maybe you can find a good associate for Barbado Investigations, you know, another set of eyes, somebody she doesn't know."

"Well, that's possible. As a matter of fact, I had an inquiry from a guy at the State Police just the other day. He's retiring next week. He might be right for the job."

"By the way," I said. "I don't suppose he's going to take the lid off Hawkins."

"Not a chance. We have to use our own shovels on this one. He's just given us permission to dig. Hey, Leo. You know what? We've got time for a couple of cold ones. There's a bar right near the Copper Tea Kettle on Court Street. I'm buying."

Chapter Fourteen

Jared was talking on the kitchen phone when DeeDee walked in and pulled some beer and sodas out of the fridge. She began packing a cooler.

"No special reason for the call, Sid. I just wanted to see how you're doing, that's all. Got to keep in touch with good business associates. Hey, I'm getting ready for some beach time, so I got to go. I'll let you know if any good deals come up. Talk later."

It was a so-so beach day, and Judy didn't feel like going with Jared and DeeDee. So the two drove over to Dennis in DeeDee's car and parked along Shore Road, at an undeveloped piece of shoreline on the Bay side, with only a couple of small cottages. A short walk over the sand took them to the cliff's edge, about thirty feet high overlooking Cape Cod Bay. The tide was in, but the water was very shallow. This was the flats. Some say you can walk out a mile at low tide and only be up to your waist.

DeeDee and Jared carried their blankets, towels, a cooler, a bag of books, suntan lotion, radio and DeeDee's purse down a long wooden stairway. The beach was empty as far as the eye could see in either direction. It was just after eleven o'clock. They turned left at the bottom of the stairs, walked about one-hundred feet and staked claim to a smooth spot of sand, spreading out a blanket. They weighted the corners of the blanket down with their sandals, the bag and the radio. Jared took out a tube of lotion and looked at DeeDee, who stripped off her tight cutoff Levi shorts and T-shirt. Her yellow bikini top showed two full breasts trying to get out. The bottom was brief, cut high up on the hips. Jared wore cutoff blue jeans, which he kept on while flipping off his sandals and peeling off his T-shirt.

"Shall I rub you down with this?" asked Jared, holding the tube up at shoulder height.

"No, not yet. Let's go in the water first."

Jared shrugged and said nothing. He watched DeeDee walk to the water and stroll in without hesitation. She eventually got up to her waist, but as she continued out, the waterline stayed about the same on her body. Jared headed in and she stopped to wait for him. He caught up to her and kept going. His six foot frame was about eight inches taller than DeeDee, so it took him longer to reach waist height in the water. Then he stopped and turned back to face his lady. She eventually reached him, but had to struggle a bit against the deeper water.

"I didn't think you were ever going to stop," she said as she jumped against him, throwing her arms around his neck.

"Just waiting for the right time," he said, wrapping both arms around her. He held her against him with his left arm; her feet didn't touch bottom. He kissed her and made it last. DeeDee's hand caressed the back of Jared's neck. He held her tighter with his left arm and slipped his right hand down the back of her bikini.

"Oh, you're such an ass man."

"That's 'cause you've got such a great ass."

Suddenly, Jared released her, grabbed her bikini bottom with both hands, and then yanked it down her legs. DeeDee giggled and stepped out of it. Jared tossed it onto his shoulder, backed away from DeeDee and started walking toward the shore.

"Hey, Buster, I'm going to need that thing."

"You can get it back." Jared never looked back as he went to the blanket and lay down. He stayed face down for a minute and then decided he'd teased DeeDee enough. He turned to get up and then burst out in laughter. DeeDee was only a few feet away, naked except for the bikini top, running toward him. She dove onto her stomach on the blanket and propped her head up with her hands.

"Say, you mind putting that back on me?"

"Not at all, my lady, not at all. But not right now."

"Wha?"

DeeDee felt Jared's hands on her hips as he turned her over. He slipped his pants off and mounted her, pulling half of the blanket over their bodies.

56

"You think we'll get into the Guinness Book of Records for this?" she asked.

"Maybe the Cape Cod Book of Records, first couple to get laid on this beach, at least in the daytime."

"Ahah! Don't count on it."

Their love making was slow. When it was over, Jared started to roll off of DeeDee and pushed the blanket off his back. Then he was startled to see a woman standing next to them. He pulled the blanket back.

"You two having fun?" It was Judy Black. "I was bored back at the house so I decided to catch up with you." She pointed back at the cliff. "Up there, I saw this blanket moving. I thought a big turtle was trying to escape or something."

They all laughed. Jared slipped the bikini back onto DeeDee and she wiggled her hips so he could get it up to its proper position. Then he put his shorts back on.

"You know, Jared, I'm going to have to put you and Scott in a Man's Best Butt contest. It'd be close."

"I'd win, hands down."

"Or hands on," said DeeDee. They laughed again.

Jared put his sunglasses on, so DeeDee couldn't see his eyes as he watched Judy strip down to her bathing suit, a red one-piece cut very low in the back. It was snug and brief on the bottom. She walked over to DeeDee and lay down next to her, facing them.

"If I knew this beach included a side show, I'd come here every day."

"Not something you can count on," said Jared.

"I guess I'll just follow you two."

Jared grabbed the tube of suntan lotion and stood up. "Time for me to save the ladies from sunburn. Judy, can I do you the favor first?"

"Hmm, sounds good to me."

"Go for it, kiddies," said DeeDee.

"You'll get yours in a minute," said Jared.

"Hah! I already got mine."

Jared took his sweet time rubbing the girls with lotion. When he announced that he was done, Judy took the tube and motioned for Jared to lie down.

"Allow me," she said. Jared complied. DeeDee made a fake snoring sound.

57

The three young people lay, quietly absorbing the sun for several minutes before Jared spoke. "Anybody want a beer?"

"I'll take one," said Judy.

"Soda for me," said DeeDee. "I packed some Pepsi in the cooler."

"There goes your reputation, Dee," said Judy.

"What's that supposed to mean?"

Judy just giggled a response while Jared opened the drinks for all. They sat in a row facing the ocean, as if they were posing like the three monkeys. The cold drinks tasted good.

"What's the new bartender like?" asked Judy.

"He's just some older guy that Ed Conley knows. Must be fifty. He's okay."

"Does anyone miss Manny?"

"No!" said Jared before DeeDee could answer.

"That's kinda cold," said Judy.

"Well, you asked, and I told you."

DeeDee held a silent, straight face.

"Well, he's not around to snuggle up to you here at the beach anymore," said Jared.

"He didn't snuggle up to me. We were friends, that's all. Hey, he never put suntan lotion on me," said DeeDee.

Jared raised an eyebrow. "Good thing."

"Hey, hey," said Judy. "Everybody just calm down. Sorry I brought it up."

"I think I'll take a walk," said DeeDee.

Judy glanced at Jared. "I'll come with you."

Jared finished his beer and lay back down. He watched the girls walk.

† † † †

The two girls strolled along the shore for a while. Judy picked up a stone and skimmed it over the water, trying to break the silence with some activity.

"I'm sorry, Dee. I was just asking about the guy. I didn't know it was a sensitive subject with Jared."

"Me neither," said DeeDee.

"Well, like I said, I'm sorry."

"The fact of the matter is, Jared is a little bit bigoted."

"Really? I've never noticed that."

"I know him better than you. I mean, I don't think he's a screaming racist or anything, like an Archie Bunker. But sometimes, he makes subtle remarks."

"Oh, like what?"

"I can't remember anything specific, but, you know, remarks, that's all."

They walked some more. Judy fell a few steps behind DeeDee. As she skipped along to catch up, she noticed a mark on DeeDee's upper back, on the left side above her shoulder blade.

"You've got a scratch there. What happened?"

"Ah, I don't know. I never knew I had it. Could have gotten it on the beach."

"It's an inch or so long."

"Is it bleeding?"

"No. It looks old. Must be a few days now."

"It's nothing. Just forget it."

Chapter Fifteen

Jared drove DeeDee back to her house, with Judy Black following right behind. Dee had put her Levis and T-shirt back on and Jared glanced often at her tanned legs as they drove.

"Still mad at me?" asked Jared.

"I wasn't mad at you. I wish Manny's name never came up, that's all. He's gone, done, over with. Poor guy." DeeDee pressed herself close to Jared and stroked his leg casually.

"Did I ever tell you you've got great legs?"

"Well, let's see, not since yesterday."

He took his right hand off the steering wheel and patted DeeDee's thigh. Then he slipped his arm around her shoulders, hugging her closer. He steered with one hand, enjoying the ride. When Dee's hand pressed against his cutoffs he enjoyed it more.

"Maybe I should speed up."

DeeDee giggled.

Jared looked in his rear view mirror to see if Judy was still behind them. She was. They were on Lower County Road, near Sea View Playland, but there was no other traffic. He began turning the wheel, making wide arcs in the road.

"Hey, stop that. What are you doing, Jared?"

"Just having some fun with Judy."

"She's going to think I'm doing you right here in the car. Stop it."

Jared laughed, made one last arc, and then settled into his proper lane just as a car approached from the other direction. He pressed a little harder on the gas pedal.

They reached the house and parked one behind the other in the driveway. They grabbed their beach things and went inside, Jared holding the door for the young ladies.

"You guys want the shower first?" Judy asked.

Jared and DeeDee looked at each other. "Naw, you go ahead Judy. We can wait," said Jared.

"I guess you can," said Judy. She broke into a tight smile.

"Or we could make it a threesome, you know, to save water," said Jared.

DeeDee slapped Jared's shoulder hard. "Cut that out, mister." She carried her things into the bedroom.

Jared looked over at Judy and held out both hands, palms up. "Sorry, kid. Not this time."

Judy shrugged her shoulders and started to walk toward her bedroom. After two steps, she turned and saw Jared walking after Dee, but looking back at her. He saw her wink.

Jared stood next to the bed and kicked off his sandals. He felt DeeDee's arms from behind him as she peeled off his T-shirt. Her hands caressed his bare chest and she pressed her body against his back.

"I love you so much, Jared. You know I do, don't you?"

"Of course I do, baby. You know it."

"I couldn't stand it if we weren't together. I need you to love me, too. You're everything to me."

"I know, baby. I love you, too."

Jared smiled as she groped for his zipper and got it down. Then she pulled his pants down to his ankles and he stepped out of them. She rubbed his buttocks and legs and then reached around to his front. Her fingers glided over his penis and in a few seconds he was fully erect. He slid away from her grasp and crawled onto the bed, turning onto his back. He smiled at DeeDee and watched her strip. She mounted him, not speaking, and she began moving slowly on top of him. After a short while, her movement became more rapid and she began to sigh. In an explosive moment, it was over.

DeeDee lay down next to Jared and ran her hand over his chest. He kissed her cheek and then lay back, eyes closed.

"Jared, I love you. Finding you has been the greatest thing to happen to me. That's why I've applied for a job at Cape Cod Hospital. If I get it, and I think I will, then I won't have to leave the Cape in September. We'll always be together."

"Oh. Yeah. That'll be great, hon. You know, I need to get some sleep before my shift starts. You should, too."

DeeDee clung to Jared for a moment and then fell asleep. Jared lay on his back staring at the ceiling.

Chapter Sixteen

It was late afternoon and Jared had just started his shift at the Chicken Roost. He was cleaning glasses behind the bar when an unexpected customer came in and grabbed the first stool, sliding his skinny frame onto the seat. He had short cropped hair, wore dark jeans rolled up at the cuff, a red T-shirt and black leather motorcycle boots, even though he didn't ride a bike. A long tattoo of a snake ran down his left arm to the elbow. His right arm had a tattoo of a mermaid surrounded by red flowers. He ordered a beer and drank from the bottle. Jared made out the tattooed letters on each knuckle except the thumb, both hands, *h-a-r-d*.

Jared looked around the empty lounge before speaking. "What are you doing here? Aren't you supposed to be keeping a distance?"

Red shirt didn't look up. "Time to check up, ya know," he said.

"No, I don't know. Why don't you get lost?"

"Now, now, that's no way to talk to a brother in arms, now, is it?"

"You've got a big mouth for someone with such a small brain."

"Ya know, Mr. Wilkes, one of these days someone's going to teach you a lesson in good manners. Perhaps it'll be me."

Jared smiled and wiped a highball glass. "I can't wait for school to begin. Finish your beer and get out of here before someone sees you."

"Not until I give you a message from Doc. He wants to see you soon, tomorrow, to be precise. Get to the shop by ten. No questions. Just do it."

Jared understood. He wiped another glass. Red shirt put his money on the bar, spun off the stool and strutted out to a dark green, beat up Chevy Nova. It looked like the finish was down to the primer paint. Jared watched him leave, then picked up the money and put it in his pocket. He went to the small fridge behind the bar and grabbed a bottle of water, opened it and took a swallow. He hadn't thought he'd have to make contact again this soon.

The morning was misty, and Jared had to run the intermittent wipers on his Opel Cadet as he cruised along the Mid-Cape Highway, over the bridge and up Route 3 to Marshfield. What was Doc up to?

Jared took the exit for Route 139 heading east. He drove about one mile before seeing the turn-in to the shop, a corrugated iron building set well off the road. The dirt driveway led to a paved parking lot with two other cars and a black pickup truck. Jared parked beside the truck and went inside. He entered an unmanned reception area that had a desk, a chair behind it and two chairs backed against the facing wall. Behind the desk was an open door. A closed door on the far left led to the shop area. There was a smell of motor oil and tires.

"Good morning, Mr. Wilkes. Come in." The voice, with a slight British cockney accent, came from the office. Doc was sitting at a gray metal desk in the corner, up against the wall. There were two eight-by-ten-inch pictures on the wall above the desk: one of the Beatles and one of Adolph Hitler. A large swastika hung above the pictures. The other walls were bare, painted green. He was in a brown swivel chair and spun around to greet Jared as he entered. He didn't get up.

Doc wore a blue Mod suit, trim cut, similar to the one Jared owned. His red shirt was open at the collar, with no necktie. His jacket hung on a coat rack beside the desk.

"Pull up a chair, Mr. Wilkes." Doc sat with his legs crossed and his hands folded.

Jared grabbed a small wooden chair against the wall and set it down facing Doc, easing himself onto it. He sat feet slightly apart, his hands on his knees.

"We seem to have a situation on our hands. Care to tell me about it?"

"I think I know where this is going," said Jared. "I can tell you up front that I don't know anything about it."

"Oh, please, Mr. Wilkes. A murder takes place in Dennis that bears a marked similarity to a job of ours last year in Needham, one that was botched. The brother who failed us has been relocated, but we're all keeping a low profile. Now, are you doing some freelance work in Dennis? I don't want you doing that. It could draw unwanted attention. You surely don't think I'm going to believe that it could be a coincidence?"

"You can believe anything you want. The Needham thing was in the Boston newspapers. Anybody could have read about it and copied the idea."

"A copycat? That's possible, Mr. Wilkes, but it's a stretch of one's imagination."

"Like I said, believe whatever you want. I'm not doing any freelance. We have a mission here and I'm true to that."

"I hope so, Mr. Wilkes. The client didn't take too well to getting the wrong man in Needham. I had to pay them back the upfront money. They think the FBI is protecting the target, so we won't get a second chance at him. You're supposed to stay on the Cape and keep low. Slashing away at niggers doesn't qualify as keeping low."

Jared stared at Doc. "I'm doing what you said to do."

"Look, Mr. Wilkes, we've got a . . . as you said, a mission and we can't afford screw ups. Our client could be a good source of money for us. I'm negotiating with the client again. We need cash for our cause. I'm hoping they'll give us another chance, but right now I can't count on that. Time will tell."

Jared's fingers closed into fists on his knees.

"Go back home, Mr. Wilkes, and do stay low. But keep your eyes and ears open a bit, in case you can learn about this . . . copycat of yours. And keep cool."

Jared stood up, stared a moment at Doc and walked out. He was cool.

Chapter Seventeen

Sometimes the only way to make progress in a case is to keep hacking away at it until something gives.

I decided to talk again with Wilkes's girlfriend and her pal, so I drove over to their place just before noon. It was a warm and slightly overcast day. The clouds hadn't burned off, so the beach wasn't good yet for working on a tan. There was a good chance the girls would be home.

Judy Black answered the door wearing a short, blue terrycloth robe. She didn't seem surprised to see me.

"Hello, Detective. Nice to see you again."

"Yes . . . ah, mind if I come in? I'd like to talk to you and Miss O'Hare about Manny Duarte."

"I thought you'd be back. Maybe I watch too much television. You know how Colombo just keeps going back to talk, over and over. DeeDee's not here. She said she had some errands to run."

"That's okay, Miss Black. I need to talk to you, too."

We stepped into the living room and I sat down in a chair. Judy curled up on her side on the sofa, propping her elbow on the arm rest and tucking her legs up. The robe crept up to mid-thigh. I still liked her tan.

"Miss Black, do you and Miss O'Hare live together during the off season?"

"Oh, call me Judy, please. Yes, we share an apartment in Norwood, a nice townhouse. We just took it last year in September. We're going to keep it again this year."

"Just the two of you?"

"No, there's another girl, Karen Fielding. She's not much of a Cape Cod person, so she's staying there by herself during the summer. She didn't want to try for a leave of absence, like DeeDee."

I had my notepad out and scribbled Karen's name in it. "What's the address and phone there, Judy?"

Judy gave me the address and started on driving directions, as if she assumed I'd be going there. "That's okay, Judy. I'm sure I can find it if I ever need to."

"Oh, yeah sure. It's just kind of instinct, you know, to give people directions. At least I always seem to do that. Sorry." She gave me the phone number.

"How do you know Karen Fielding?"

"DeeDee and Karen both work at Norwood Hospital. They're nurses. It was DeeDee's idea to ask her to share the apartment with us. She's real nice, so we became friends easy."

"What's she like?"

"Like I said, she's real nice. Kind of quiet, you know. DeeDee's the real outgoing one. I'm kind of in-between, I guess. Depends on who's around. Sometimes I can let it all hang out, you know, if I'm comfortable with the crowd."

Judy's robe inched up higher. I guess she was feeling comfortable.

"Did any of you ladies have any friends or contacts in Needham?"

"Ah, come to think of it, Karen worked at the hospital there . . . the Glover. She was on some sort of a loan out, you know, where she works at another hospital for a while when they're short on nurses."

"Do you remember when that was?"

"Oh yeah, last fall, for three months. Excuse me, Detective, I don't mean to sound rude or anything, but what's this all got to do with Manny and all?"

"Maybe nothing, but I've got to try to get as broad a picture of this as I can. Does Karen ever come to visit you here?"

"Like I said, she's not crazy about the Cape for some reason, so she doesn't come down much. She came down early in the summer for a weekend. Maybe she'll come down for Labor Day if she gets time off. I doubt it."

"Did she come alone?"

"Yeah. She's got a boyfriend but they're not too serious. She said it was a girl's night out sort of weekend for her that time. I hope she comes back. We had fun. Scott had one of his buddies with him and he sort of paired off with Karen. It was cool."

Cool? I bet it got rather hot. To be young. It was sure different from when Natalie and I were young. We were in love. Today, these kids just seem to be in heat.

"Can I get you anything, Detective, a cold drink, coffee?"

"No, I'm good, thanks. Besides, I'll be leaving now. You've been very cooperative. Thanks. You still have my number, right?

"Oh yes, your card is in my purse." Judy got up from the sofa slowly.

"If you think of anything at all, *anything,* please call me."

"Of course, Detective."

"I'll try to catch DeeDee O'Hare at another time."

Judy walked to the front door as I walked out. As I got back to my car, I looked toward the house, I saw Judy watching me from the door. She smiled and waved. I wondered if any of my teachers had spent their summers on the Cape and walked around in skimpy robes.

I drove back to the office and called Leo.

"What gives, Jack? Got any hot news?"

"No, not exactly hot. I just found out from Judy Black that she and DeeDee O'Hare share an apartment during the off season with a woman named Karen Fielding. They live in Norwood. Karen's a nurse, like O'Hare and works at Norwood Hospital. Seems she worked a detail at the Glover Hospital in Needham for a while last fall. It's not much, but why don't you check her out?"

"That's such a bad straight line, Jack, that I won't even honor it with a punch line."

"That's good, Leo, because you're much too old for these young ones."

"I may have age, but I also have wisdom and experience."

"You also have an ex-wife and an alimony payment every month."

"Jack, Jack, Jack, can't you look on the brighter side of things once in a while?"

"As soon as we solve this case, old pal. Now get cracking and see what gems of knowledge she has about Needham, since she worked there when that murder took place."

I gave Leo the address and phone number. It wasn't exactly a lead in the case, but it was worth sending out my bloodhound.

Chapter Eighteen

I was in the office at headquarters when my desk phone rang, about two-thirty. It was probably Natalie with something from her honey-do list.

"Hello, Detective Contino? This is Millie Wallenski, a waitress at the Beachgoer."

"Yes, of course, Miss Wallenski, what can I do for you?" Another bad guess for me.

"Well, I've been thinking about Manny a lot and wondering if there was anything that you should know about. I really couldn't think straight the night you told me about Manny."

"I understand, Miss Wallenski. Is there something you remember now?"

"Well, one night at work, before it got busy, we were standing at the bar, me, DeeDee and Manny. We were just chatting and Manny was flirting with DeeDee. She didn't seem to mind. Well, Manny said something about going to the race track at Foxboro on his night off with his cousin, Pete. He went on about his cousin, like he was sort of a big brother to Manny. I guess he's a couple of years older. Manny said he works as an orderly at the Needham hospital."

"What's Pete's last name? Do you know?"

"Yeah, it's also Duarte. I guess Manny really liked being with him whenever he could. Like I said, it seemed that Manny thought of him as an older brother type."

"What else did Manny say about his cousin?"

"He said he was tall and good looking, that the ladies really went for him. Manny thought he was a real stud, you know."

"Did you ever meet him?"

"No, I don't recall him ever coming to the restaurant."

"What about DeeDee? Did she know him?"

"I don't think so. Besides, she said she had something to do and walked away at that point, so Manny just talked to me for a while."

"Do you know where Pete lives?"

"I believe he's in Fall River."

"That's a long commute."

"Yeah. I guess Needham pays more so he doesn't mind the trip."

"Is there anything else, Miss Wallenski?"

"That's all I can think of right now. I know it's not much, but, well, Manny didn't seem to know too many guys, but when I remembered his talking about his cousin, I thought I should mention it to you. I hope I didn't bother you with this."

"Not at all, Miss Wallenski. I'm glad you called. Always feel free to call me anytime you think of something. We never know what bit of information will help out."

"Okay, Detective. Thanks. Good bye."

"Good bye, Miss Wallenski."

It was starting to look like a productive day after all. At least the geographic circle was beginning to widen in this case. It stretched off Cape to include Fall River, Norwood and Needham. Maybe it was just coincidence, but Karen Fielding, a friend of Judy and DeeDee, worked a detail in a hospital where Manny's cousin worked. *Funny, the Duartes didn't mention Cousin Pete to me. Maybe there's a reason why.*

I waited until early evening to call the Duartes to tell them that I'd like to see them again. They were agreeable, so I hopped in my car and drove to their modest house. I never got used to calling on the family of a murder victim, especially the parents.

Andrew and Tina Duarte were hard-working, shy people who were stunned by their son's death. A short time had passed since they buried him. I could only imagine the pain.

Tina greeted me at the door and led me to their living room where Andrew was standing. We shook hands politely and sat down. They took the sofa together and I parked myself in a corner easy chair. Tina offered me coffee, but I declined.

71

"I've recently learned that Manny has a cousin named Pete who he was very fond of. I can't help but wonder why you didn't mention him to me before." There. I got it out.

The Duartes looked at each other without speaking. Then Andrew began wringing his hands as he turned toward me. "I'm sorry, Detective. When we met before, we were still very upset and shocked. I guess we just weren't prepared for answering a lot of questions. Believe me, we meant no harm. I'm sorry for the oversight."

"That's okay, Andrew. I understand."

The Duartes permitted me to use their first names. They felt more comfortable that way. I tried to extend the same courtesy, but they always addressed me as Detective.

"Is there anything I should know about Pete?"

Once again, they looked at each other before Andrew looked at me. "Please try to understand that although our family ties are strong, my nephew Peter is not high on our list of favorites. My brother, his father, died when he was a young boy. His mother worked hard and did her best to raise him, but he was very hurt when his father died and he became sullen and angry. He took to a bad crowd as a teenager and got into trouble a lot. He wasn't a criminal, but he had some minor scrapes with the law."

I interrupted at that point. "Excuse me, Andrew. What types of problems did he have with the law?"

"Mostly drunk and disorderly, brawling in public places, things like that. His mother feared that he smoked pot, but he's never been caught. We didn't like it when he visited because we were afraid he'd be a bad influence on Manny."

"So Pete never had a serious criminal record, just some drunk and disorderly."

"That's correct. But I fear he may have gotten away with more than that. He hung around with some less than desirable people, you know. Fortunately, he went into the service after school and I think that helped him. But he never developed a career path. He just seems to look for jobs that he can handle, nothing requiring any skills or training. He isn't like Manny."

"I understand that he works in Needham, at the Glover Hospital. That's a long way to go for a job."

"Yes, he rides with two other guys who have jobs up there. They both work at a garage in Needham. Peter prefers the hospital. He says there aren't any pretty babes in garages."

"Can you give me Pete's address and phone number? I might want to talk to him."

Tina seemed startled. "You don't think he had anything to do with Manny's death, do you?"

"No, no, Tina. I just need to know as much as possible about Manny's friends and acquaintances. It's just routine."

"Sure, we understand," said Andrew, nodding as he took Tina's hand. "Tina, write down Peter's information for Detective Contino, please." He released her hand and she left the room. "Peter also likes to gamble; race tracks, Jai alai, poker, you know, stuff like that. He wanted to get Manny to join in with him. I cautioned Manny against it, but he said it was all legal and he found it exciting. He said he didn't go with Peter very often. He really didn't have the free time, so going once in a while couldn't hurt. That's what he said."

Tina came back with a slip of paper, folded it once and slipped it to me.

"Thank you for your time. I'm sorry to have to bother you like this."

"That's okay, Detective. We want to help you catch whoever did this to our son, so feel free to call us if you need to."

I nodded, tucked the paper into my shirt pocket and walked to the front door with Andrew alongside. As we got to the door, Andrew spoke softly to me. "Detective, Peter is family, even if I do think he was a bad influence. I can't believe he would be mixed up in this, but if he is, please, I need to know."

"Of course, Andrew, but like I explained, I just need to get all the information I can. Thanks again, and good night."

"Good night, Detective."

A guy, like a rotten apple, can spoil those around him. I've seen it happen to families before.

I drove home, greeted Natalie, who was watching television, and went into the dining room to pour myself a bourbon. I reached into the cabinet and grabbed a glass. It was solid with a strong base that felt good in my hand. I took it into the kitchen for ice. I liked the solid sound of three cubes dropping into it, like the sound a baseball makes when a hitter gets good wood on the ball. Bringing it back to the liquor cabinet, I thought about the Duartes and what they must be going through. It had been a long day and I was tired, so I made it a double.

I looked at the pictures of our kids on the hutch. Jim graduated from UMass Medical School in 1975 and was doing his residency at Massachusetts General Hospital. Annie, our oldest, was a high school English teacher working on her Master's. No rotten apples in this family.

I made my way back to the living room and stood near the sofa where Nat was sitting, watching an old Bogart movie. "Got room there for an old cop?"

She patted the empty cushion next to her without looking away from the TV, so I lowered myself onto it. I put the drink down on the coffee table in front of us, kicked my shoes off, stretched out my legs, feet on the table, and grabbed my refreshment, easing myself comfortably next to Nat. She was watching *Casablanca*.

"Did they round up the usual suspects yet?" I asked?

"No, did you?"

"I wish I had some usual ones. I've just got some lying kid with a racism problem." I held up my drink and winked at Nat. "Here's looking at you, kid."

Chapter Nineteen

Leo decided it was time to enlist some help. He and Jack needed to keep an eye on Agent Tammy Watson and now there was this Karen Fielding to check up on. He had a feeling there would be more characters in this investigation soon, so, a call to a sergeant at the Framingham State Police barracks was in order. He got through to Sergeant Leary, who was retiring soon, and set up a personal appointment at Barbado Investigations.

Skip Leary was an athletic-looking six footer in his early forties. He had known Leo and Jack on a professional basis for many years. He admired them for their work against organized crime. With retirement starting soon and college bills looming, he was glad that Leo took him up on his request for part time work to supplement his pension. He entered Leo's office wearing pressed gray slacks, a white shirt, red tie and blue blazer.

"Geeze, Skip, you're a bit formal looking for this office. Most guys come by in khakis and a golf shirt, at best."

"Always want to make the right impression on a job interview, Leo. It's important."

"What job interview? You've got the job if you want it. I just got to explain a few things, that's all."

"Oh, well, that's great, Leo. Go ahead. What have you got, a runaway, a cheating husband?"

Leo sat at his desk, hands palms down on it. He began tapping his right index finger on the desk surface. "Skip, I know you were in the military. You know what Top Secret means, right?"

"Yeah, sure. So this is something big, or at least sensitive."

"Skip, when you're working on my clock, you have to put that work at the top of your list, no matter what. I was a MET, so I know what it means to be on the public pay-roll. I may ask you to do things that you can't talk about to anyone. Nothing illegal, mind you, but Top Secret as far as we're concerned. You can't talk to anybody."

Skip swallowed hard. "You're serious about this."

"Very serious, Skip."

"Say, how much does this job pay? No. Forget that."

"We'll talk about that later. Let's just say while on a pension, Barbado Investigations helps me with alimony payments and car insurance. So, if the boss asks, you can tell him what kind of work you're doing and that it's with me. Just keep mum about the actual case."

"Okay. I understand. I can handle that, Leo. What are the details?"

Leo explained the situation about the FBI, Agent Tammy Watson, the State Police and the Needham murder case. Skip Leary turned pale.

"Wow. That sounds pretty . . . involved. The FBI is keeping the Needham PD in the cold."

"They want to keep the circle pretty tight around this case. They think it's small potatoes, but could lead them to something bigger. The fewer noses digging into it, the less likely any leaks will be sprung. Even your boss, Major Hawkins, can't talk about it. I know that because another source told me. So you see, sometimes people in our own business have to turn a cold shoulder to others, even though they trust them. That's why as an investigator for me you'd have to live by the ground rules I just told you about."

"I'm good with that, Leo. What can I do?"

"I need you to help me by keeping an eye on Agent Watson for a short while."

"You think she's dirty?"

"Maybe. Maybe not. She's supposed to be working undercover snooping on Sammy White and Tommy Shea. Problem is, we think she's too buddy-buddy with White, maybe both of them. If she's having sleep-overs with White, then she's extending her courageous tour of duty a bit too far. I want you to follow her. See where she goes and who she's with. It may mean camping out in your car. Can you handle that? Can your wife handle that?"

"I can handle it. My wife can, too. She knows I want a part time job with you and she knows it could mean some long hours. She's a strong girl. She'll be fine."

Leo stood up to signal that the talk was over and walked Skip to the door. "Too bad my ex never could handle long cop hours. That's why wives like mine become ex. Wives like yours and Jack's become Grandma."

Chapter Twenty

It was a warm, sunny day; a great beach day by any accounts, but Jared and DeeDee had their distractions—the usual one for young couples during the summer on the Cape. Late nights meant late mornings.

Jared touched DeeDee's back lightly as they lay in bed, DeeDee on her right side with her back to him. The light pressure on her back woke her, as intended. His strong hand caressed her spine, then moved down to her lower back, then lower. He pushed the covers away so he could enjoy the full view of her beautiful body, head to foot. His hand lingered on her left buttock and then continued its journey, brushing her leg down past her knee, over her calf and on to her heel. Slowly, his hand retraced its trip.

Jared continued the slow hand motion until she smiled and turned over to face him, snuggling up close to his side as he stretched out on his back. They said nothing. He enjoyed the feel of DeeDee's left hand on his chest and the circle she began to trace on it. She snuggled closer, and Jared could feel her warm breath on his skin. After a while, DeeDee expanded the circle her hand was tracing over Jared's chest. He noticed.

The circle got larger, running from Jared's chest to his abdomen. The anticipation got to him as her hand circled back to his chest. On its next pass over his abdomen, her hand bumped into the masculine object blocking its path. She slid her fingers around it, stroking it, then gripping it tightly. DeeDee smiled at Jared, giggled softly and then mounted him, taking him inside. He placed his hands on her hips to guide her rhythmic motion, then one hand moved to her breasts.

DeeDee's excitement grew and she moaned in pleasure. Jared was stoic, his mouth closed. He continued touching her and finally she climaxed, her head back, turning from side to side, her mouth emitting a muffled groan.

"Are you exercising self-control?" she asked in a breathless tone.

"Trying to." Jared answered through gritted teeth. In seconds, his mouth opened full and his control was lost. They smiled at each other as DeeDee moved off him and resumed her position beside him. They stayed that way and dozed off again.

Jared awoke after a short, sound sleep and noticed he was alone. The sound of running water from the bathroom told him where DeeDee was. He decided to use the outside shower behind the house.

When he finished, Jared dried off quickly, threw his towel over one shoulder and walked back into the house through the kitchen door. He didn't expect to see Judy making coffee. She didn't expect to see a naked man walking through the kitchen. Neither was startled, however.

"You know, that outside shower feels great," he said, without breaking his stride toward the bedroom.

"I'll bet it does," said Judy, eyeballing his tall figure while she wiped a coffee mug with a dishtowel.

"You ought to try it sometime."

"Maybe I will." Her hands gripped the mug tightly.

Jared wrapped the towel around himself as he approached the bedroom, then entered. DeeDee was dressed in blue cutoff shorts and a red tank top. "Is Judy up? I thought I heard you two talking."

"Yeah, I was just telling her how great that outdoor shower is. She's making coffee."

"Good. I could use some. Let me just go put on my face and I'll be right back."

Jared dropped the towel and went to the dresser, where he kept some of his clothes. He got dressed and then walked into the bathroom, slipping past DeeDee at the double sink. He lathered his face, grabbed a razor and began shaving as DeeDee finished her makeup. In a couple of minutes, the two were in the kitchen having coffee with Judy.

"Anybody having breakfast?" asked Judy.

"Breakfast? It's almost lunchtime." Jared shook his head. He poured coffee for himself and DeeDee.

"The coffee is breakfast," laughed DeeDee. "Hey, let's go out to that little place in Harwich on the corner of Bank Street and Route 28. I think they serve breakfast all day, so we can't lose."

"Mind if I come along?" asked Judy.

"Of course not," said DeeDee. "I was asking both of you anyway."

"Certainly," added Jared. "Bring your little tush along."

Judy smiled.

"Boy, have you got a one track mind, Jared," said DeeDee.

"Yes, but at least it's on the right track."

DeeDee slapped him on the shoulder.

The three finished their coffee and headed to the driveway. They looked at the cars and then at each other.

"Jared," said Judy. "You'd better drive with DeeDee up front. I'll take the back seat. If I drive, then you two will sit in the back together playing feely touchy."

Jared glared at her. "And your point is?"

They laughed and turned to DeeDee's car. Jared already had her keys from the night before. "You know, Judy, sometimes I think you'd make a perfect stranger."

"Hardee har-har," mocked Judy. "Get in the car and drive."

In about ten minutes they were pulling into the parking lot at the Bank Street Diner. Jared saw a spot to his liking in the back row against the short hedges that lined the lot, pulled DeeDee's car up, but turned away from it, pulling forward just a bit so that he could back in. Just as he put the car into reverse and turned to look over his shoulder, a small Toyota Corolla darted in from out of nowhere and pulled nose-first into the spot.

"What the hell!" Jared was livid. He got out of the car and rushed over to the Toyota.

A thin, medium-build Black man got out. He was in his mid-thirties, wearing gray slacks and a white shirt with the sleeves rolled up at the cuff.

"What do you think you're doing?" shouted Jared, getting into the man's face. "I was taking that spot."

"You snooze, you lose, pal. I got there first."

The veins in Jared's neck were bulging. "Move that foreign car!"

80

DeeDee ran up to Jared and grabbed his arm. "Please, Jared, it's okay. There are other spaces."

"That's not the point." Jared never took his eyes off the Black man.

"I obviously got there first, because my car is in the space," said the man. He walked away holding his arms out to his sides, palms up.

"Don't walk away from me, Sambo!"

"Jared, please. Don't. It's not worth it." DeeDee tugged harder on his arm. "We can park in another spot. Come on. Let's eat."

"Not here," snapped Jared. "Being in the same room with that Black bastard will spoil my appetite. We'll go someplace else."

"Okay, Jared, but please, do you have to talk like that?"

"What, you're going to lecture me?"

"No, of course not. It's just that, well, I don't like to hear you like that."

Jared walked back to the car and opened the door. As he did, he looked at Judy in the back seat. She looked back at Jared with a slight smile across her closed lips. When they were all back in the car, Jared drove them to another diner. It was a silent drive and a quiet meal.

Jared's anger fueled his resolve. His mission was clear.

Chapter Twenty-One

Logging miles in the car is part of the business when you're a cop and a private investigator. Leo accepted this fact, even if it did get to be a pain sometimes. This particular afternoon it meant driving to Norwood Hospital to check up on Karen Fielding. When he found out that she wasn't due in until the three-thirty shift, it meant adding a few more miles going across town to her apartment. Jack had provided the address after a talk with Judy Black. Jack also told him about Peter Duarte.

The apartment complex, just off Route 1A, was fairly new and looked a whole lot better than anything Leo knew about when he was in his twenties. He parked in the designated visitor's space, walked up to the ground level entrance, rang the bell and waited. In a minute, the door opened and a good looking girl with light brown hair, in short cutoffs and a tight T-shirt, looked right at him. "Can I help you?" she asked. He decided that this was a better meeting place than the hospital.

"I hope so," said Leo. "Are you Karen Fielding?"

"Yes, I am. Who are you?"

"My name is Leo Barbado. I'm a private investigator." Leo showed his ID. "I'm here because I understand that you share this apartment with Judy Black and DeeDee O'Hare."

"Yes, I do. Are they in some sort of trouble?"

"No, Miss, not exactly. May I come in?"

Karen opened the door, turned and walked past the entryway into the kitchen. She pulled out a chair at a breakfast table and eased herself onto it. Leo enjoyed her graceful movements. He took a seat at the table across from her.

"So, just what is it that Judy and Dee are involved with that calls for a private investigator?"

"A couple of weeks ago, the bartender was murdered outside the restaurant where DeeDee works."

"Yeah, I know about that. Judy called me shortly after it happened. It must have been awful. But why a private investigator? Don't the police take care of these things?"

"Yes, they do. The Chief of Detectives in Dennis has asked me to help out. You see, the murder is strikingly similar to one that happened ten months ago in Needham."

"I remember that one. I was working in Needham at the time. They don't get a lot of murders in a town like Needham, so that was big news. But what has all this got to do with Judy and DeeDee?"

"When you worked at the Glover Hospital, did you know a man named Peter Duarte?"

"Peter . . . yes, I remember him, tall fellow, handsome, nice guy, but I didn't really know him very well."

"Do you know anything about him—where he went after work, what he liked to do in his spare time, who he hung out with?"

"Like I said, Mr. Barbado, I hardly knew the guy."

"So, you didn't know that the bartender who was killed was his cousin?"

Karen's jaw hung loose for a moment. "No, I didn't know that. Boy, that's kinda weird."

"Wait," said Leo. "You talked to Judy Black about the murder and it never occurred to you that Manny Duarte might be related to Peter Duarte? Weren't you curious enough to ask?"

"I didn't know the guy's last name. She only said he was named Manny. I had no idea."

Leo looked right at her and held her gaze. "Okay," he said, finally shifting his look. "Now that you do know, think back and try to recall anything that seems like a possible connection. Maybe there's something like the guys Peter knew and what they did together. Maybe Manny hung out with them at times."

"Look, Mr. Barbado, I told you I didn't really know Peter, so I don't have any answers for you."

Leo decided to try another approach. "This is a nice apartment. How long have you and the other girls been living here?

"We moved in last September."

"You all knew each other long?"

83

"Well, I've known DeeDee since high school. I got to know Judy when we moved in."

"You and DeeDee are both nurses."

"Yes and we work together at Norwood Hospital." Karen rolled her eyes.

"But you got transferred to Glover."

"Not a transfer. It was a short detail, three months, which is how I became acquainted with Peter Duarte."

"So you know that DeeDee goes with a guy named Jared Wilkes."

"Yeah, she told me about him. I guess she's really fallen for him. I hope she's careful."

"What do you mean?"

"Like I said, I've known her since high school. DeeDee always got into intense relationships. She couldn't take the breakups, though."

"Sounds like there were a few."

"Yes, over the years. She had a couple of experiences like that, in high school, nursing school and after. The last one was real bad."

Leo folded his arms in front of him and settled in his chair, as if he expected a good story was on its way. "Please explain."

"Three years ago, DeeDee had a boyfriend named Dwayne. She loved him very much, thought he was the one and figured they'd get married. One day, he got into an accident on Route 128 and was killed instantly. It was awful. It really tore Dee up. She went into a real funk, you know, got pretty hard to get along with. About a week after the funeral, she got picked up by the cops one day at the graveside."

"What on earth for?"

Karen paused and caught her breath, as if she didn't want to go into this.

"She was kneeling at the grave, screaming at Dwayne for leaving her and digging at the ground with a garden trowel. I guess she was using it more like a knife than a garden tool and she kept screaming at him. Somebody called the cops and they took her away. She was checked in to Medfield State Hospital, you know, for the mentally disturbed. It was just a short observation. They charged her with desecrating a grave, but the charges were dropped and she was put into grief counseling for three months. She's been fine ever since."

"Holy cow. She actually brought a trowel to the grave, intending to dig it up? That doesn't sound very spontaneous. I'm surprised they dropped the charges."

"Well, she was pretty upset and when they learned the full story, you know, I mean they were almost engaged, so I guess the judge figured she was in some real pain. He felt sorry for her and realized that she was a good kid and didn't deserve to be locked up."

"She's been a peach ever since, eh?"

Karen looked irked at Leo's tone. "Yes, Mr. Barbado. She's fine. She bounced back and started seeing guys again, but she stayed away from tight relationships, until this Jared guy."

Leo decided that this was a good time to end the interview. He produced a card from his pocket and slid it across the table for her.

"That's all for now. Thank you for your time, Miss Fielding. If you think of something else that might help, call me, okay?"

"Yeah, sure." She took the card, looked at it and began tapping it lightly on the table.

"I can let myself out." He made his way slowly, noticing the tapping sound that Karen made with his card. Something in that conversation must have gotten to her.

Chapter Twenty-Two

"Hello, Leo, nice of you to call. Got anything interesting to talk about?" Most of the time Leo was pretty quiet, but now and then he could talk up a blue streak. As long as that streak was full of useful information I was okay with it.

"I'll say. I met Karen Fielding today. She's good to look at, but not exactly much help for us. She knew about Manny Duarte's killing because Judy Black called her shortly after it happened. She also doesn't know much about Cousin Petey, only knew him by acquaintance when she worked at the Glover Hospital. She didn't even know Manny's last name so she never made any connection between the two Duartes. But she told me a doozie of a story about DeeDee O'Hare."

I took in Leo's tale about DeeDee and the incident at the grave of her old boyfriend. "Hmmmm. I guess there's more to her than meets the eye. But on everything else, it's a big blank. Somehow that whole business just seems too strange. DeeDee works with Manny. She rooms with Karen Fielding, who meets Peter Duarte in Needham. There's a murder in Needham that is almost identical to Manny's killing. That's all just too coincidental, don't you think?"

"Yeah, it's a little fishy, but you know what they say, the sea is full of fish and they all stink."

"Who says that?"

"Well, I just did, for one. Look, we just got to keep pounding on this nut. Eventually, it's going to crack. We just need to find a weak spot."

"Agreed. Where are you now?"

"I'm in Norwood at a pay phone."

"Okay, call the Glover Hospital and find out when Peter Duarte is scheduled to be in. We'll pay him a visit."

"Got it, Jack."

Leo made the call and confirmed that Peter Duarte was working the day shift and would be in at eight in the morning. When he called me back, we made plans to meet at the Glover around ten the next day.

The drive off Cape was uneventful, save for a slowdown in Braintree at the junction of Route 3 and Route 128. I took the Dedham Avenue exit off the highway and drove into Needham, pulling into the parking lot in front of the Glover a few minutes before ten. I parked at the far side of the lot nearest School Street. I got out and stood beside my car so Leo could spot me. Across the street was the building that housed the Needham Police and the Fire Department. *How convenient,* I thought, *Police, Fire and Hospital all right next to each other. Very efficient town planning.*

Leo never made me wait very long. He pulled into the lot, drove up near the building and spotted me. There were several open spots, so he pulled in beside my car.

We entered the building, went to the front desk, showed our credentials and asked for Peter Duarte We were shown a seating area, but elected to stand at the desk. A couple of minutes after being paged, Peter Duarte showed up. He was almost my height wearing blue hospital scrubs. He had a white T-shirt on under the blue top. He looked familiar, but I couldn't place the face.

"You guys want to see me about something?" he asked.

"I'm Detective Jack Contino, Dennis Police Department. This is Leo Barbado, a private investigator working with us on the case."

"Really. I wasn't sure there really were private investigators. Thought that was something TV made up."

"Oh, I'm real all right," said Leo.

"Apparently. I'm going to guess that this has something to do with my cousin's murder. How can I help you?"

I motioned to the seating area and we took up positions on the small sofa and a chair at right angles to each other.

"I talked with Manny's parents and they said you were like a big brother to Manny."

"Yeah, well I tried to be. He was a good kid, but a little too serious, so I tried to get him to loosen up a bit."

"Like how?' asked Leo.

"I invited him up to my place in Fall River now and then. I introduced him to some of my friends and we'd go out together, you know, sometimes to the race track, Jai alai, poker games. He liked it."

"Peter, naturally, your relationship with Manny was different from his parents'. You might have known about things in his life that they didn't." I stopped talking and looked at Peter for a response. He looked blankly back at me, as if waiting for the right words to come.

"His folks knew he went to those places with me. I don't think they liked it, but, hey, Manny's over twenty-one, so they couldn't stop him."

"What about girls?" Leo asked.

"See, that was part of the problem," said Peter. "Manny was such a hard-working kid, tending bar and going to school, he never had much time for social life. I was trying to help him change that."

"Anybody special?" I asked.

"Well, there was this nurse at the hospital. She only worked here for a short while, but it didn't take long for me to make her acquaintance. Man, she was as hot as a pistol. Couldn't keep her hands to herself, either, if you get my drift. Look, I got the equipment, you know? Nature's been good to me. I guess she just couldn't help but notice. Next thing I know, she's all over me every chance she gets. We're doing it in the closet, in the storeroom, even in a private room that was empty. Man, she was something. Anyway, I was hoping to introduce her to Manny so he could get a little. She said she lived with a couple of other girls, so I thought we could party sometime."

Leo and I looked at each other. We spoke at the same time. "This girl got a name?" We looked at each other again.

"Karen, Karen something. Fields, or something like that."

"Fielding, maybe, Karen Fielding?" I said.

"Yeah, could be Fielding. I think so. Anyway, it never happened for Manny. See, she turned out to be a bit of an Archie Bunker type, you know. Me and my dick were good enough for her under cover, so to speak. But she didn't want anything to do with me outside of this place. Actually, I was okay with that, too, but I never admitted it to her. She wouldn't have fit in with my crowd either. I was just as happy to keep letting her clean my tubes right here. I didn't have to wine and dine her, you know. A good piece can be costly. It's like, you can go to a pro and pay for it or you can have a girlfriend and pay even more." He laughed at his own joke and slapped his thigh.

"So what happened to this . . . Karen?"

I could feel Leo's stare.

"After she went back to Norwood Hospital, that was it. She wouldn't give me her phone number, so I let it go. Too bad. Man, she had all the moves, you know. Too bad. But then, a strange deal came along. I guess Karen talked about our playtime to her buddy. This girl shows up at the Glover Hospital one day, after Karen went back to Norwood. She has me paged and I come out to meet her. I guess she wanted to see the goods in person, you know. So she tells me that she's friends with Karen and I guess she liked what she saw because she says we should go out sometime. So, eventually, we found time to get together and, I really mean get together. She's pretty hot stuff, too, like Karen. We meet a couple of times, get to a local motel, and do the thing, you know. Then she stops coming around. I guess she satisfied her curiosity about Black guys, or something. Okay with me."

"So you never saw her again, either?" I said.

"Not until Manny's funeral. I wasn't surprised to see her there. He told me once about this girl at his restaurant named DeeDee, who was a nurse in Norwood, and we put it together. I told Manny about my time with her and suggested he go after her for a good time. He liked that idea. Don't know if he ever tried her, though. Small world, huh, this hot chick winds up working with Manny on the Cape while she's on leave from the hospital. I hope he scored one with her before . . . poor guy."

Peter got up and looked at the clock on the wall across from us. "I really got to get back to work, guys. Is there anything else?"

I stood up slowly. "No, not right now. We may want to talk to you again. In the meantime, call me if you think of anything else that might be useful."

"Sure will, Detective. Sure will. You got to catch Manny's killer, man. You got to."

Peter Duarte scooted away and turned the corner.

"Leo, I thought you said Miss Fielding denied knowing this guy very well."

"Well, I guess she only knew him in the biblical sense. Other than for a toss in the laundry basket, she stayed away from the guy, so she probably thought she was telling me the truth. So, you want to go see her again?"

"If we confront her with this, she'll just apologize and clam up after that. Let's hold on to this little tidbit and wait for a better time to bring it out, if there ever is one. I think it's more interesting that DeeDee O'Hare also made his acquaintance, so to speak. I need to speak to her about this."

I told Leo to let me know as soon as he heard from the ex-State trooper he hired to watch Tammy Watson, and invited him down to the Cape for the weekend. He could bring a friend, if he wanted to. I was pretty sure he was still seeing somebody, but he didn't talk about her much. We left the hospital, Leo heading back to Somerville and me going back to Dennis.

I got back to Dennis a little after noon, so I stopped at the Kreme N'Kone to get a quick lunch. They had great fried clams and I realized that this was one of the true benefits of living here. You just don't have the same kind of atmosphere in greater Boston. Here, I could cut down on meatball subs. Clams and a beer, no harm done.

Chapter Twenty-Three

Around seven that night, the phone rang. *This better not be another surprise.* Good thing I'd restocked my liquor cabinet.

Natalie answered it in the kitchen while I was loading the dishwasher. "Oh, hi, Leo. I hear you're coming down this weekend. That's great. Oh, sure. He's right here."

I dried my hands and took the phone as Natalie left the room. "What's up, Leo?"

"I think we're starting to get close to something and they don't like it."

"How so?"

"Skip Leary, the ex-Statie I hired to watch Tammy Watson, got jumped by a couple of thugs the other night while staking out Agent Watson and Sammy White. He'd been doing it for only two nights, but they made him, somehow. They started a ruckus by his car and got him to come out. The next thing he knew he was getting hit in the ribs, must have been a third guy. When he turned around he saw a guy in jeans and a red T-shirt. Leary grabbed the guy by the throat. Next thing, the lights went out. When he woke up, some paramedics were working on him in an ambulance. They took him to Mass General. He's okay, but he took a few stitches in the scalp and may have a concussion. He's got some bruised ribs as well. Going to keep him overnight."

"Had he reported anything to you about Watson?"

"Yeah, but it was what we expected. She was keeping late company with Sammy White. He was sure she made it a sleep over. Saw her go in but never came out. This was on two separate stake outs this week."

"What about the guy in the red T-shirt, can Leary identify him?"

"Skip said it happened real fast. It was a white guy, kinda skinny and shaved head, maybe a tattoo of some kind on his arm. Really couldn't tell you about facial features, so he's not confident about making an ID from mug shots. He's down on himself for getting hit like this, but I told him we've all been there, especially when we first started doing surveillance work."

"So you figure this is definitely related to Watson and Sammy White."

"Can't see any other connection. They didn't take his weapon or any money, so robbery doesn't seem likely. Of course, maybe the thugs got spooked by something or someone and made a quick exit. But it looks like another strange coincidence to me and I don't buy it. I figure they made him at the stakeout and found out who he was. Couldn't have been too hard to do, with Agent Watson helping out. I figure they took their time getting to him, you know, to cover their tracks real good. There's no way we can prove the connection without ringing up Ms. Watson."

"I agree. But someday soon, we're going to do just that to dear Tammy. For now, I think it's time we said hello to Mr. White, just to let him know who he's dealing with. I'll meet you at your office a couple of hours, around nine."

"Got it. See you soon."

Natalie wasn't happy about me going to Boston so late, but she understood. The weather was clear and the drive was easy.

Leo and I met up and he drove into Boston, going right to Club 77, one of the spots where Sammy White liked to hang out. There was a car parked in front along the curb, the last space before an alley. Leo pulled halfway past it, blocking it and the alley. We would've bet the car belonged to the club owner, Joe Vito, a guy we'd love to see behind bars.

The bartender, a very tall guy, was talking to a customer. He looked at us as we walked in and then looked away. Then he looked back at us and straightened up. Nice to be recognized.

"You're getting a bit gray up top, Teddy boy." Leo and I knew Big Ted from way back, too. "Don't bother ringing up Mr. Vito, Ted. We're not looking for him anyway."

"What do you assholes want?"

"Now, Ted, is that any way to talk to old friends?" Leo smiled as he spoke.

I grabbed Leo by the arm and motioned to a table in the far corner. There was Sammy White, Tommy Shea and two women. One of the women was Agent Tammy Watson, diligently on the job. We went over to say hello.

"Hey, wop cop, I thought you were retired," said Shea.

"Fortunately for you, Tommy, I'm only retired from the METs. I'm still on the job." I avoided eye contact with Agent Watson.

"Yeah, I heard that. Now you're a Cape Cod wop cop. Seems you're way out of your territory, as in jurisdiction."

"Oh, you worried about something, Tommy?"

"What, me worry?" Shea laughed, slapping his thigh. "Get it, from MAD magazine?"

Sammy White just sat there. His face was taut, his hands curled into fists on the table. The girl with Tommy Shea looked scared. She didn't know what to make of this scene. She'd probably never seen anyone stand up to Shea before. Agent Watson was calm and quiet.

"You're a real comic, Tommy," I said. "You were always good for a laugh."

"Maybe someday I'll make you laugh out the other side of your face," said Shea.

"Well, I'd sure love to see you try. I can still kick your ass from here into next week."

Shea's face grew serious. He didn't respond. I knew he remembered our first encounter many years ago.

Leo decided to step in. "A friend of ours, a former State trooper, got mugged last night. You wouldn't happen to know anything about that, would you?" He looked right at Sammy White.

"Gee, I'm sorry to hear that," said Shea. "How would we know anything about that? People get mugged in this town every night. We've been entertaining these beautiful ladies since last night. Isn't that right, girls? Boy, even an ex-Statie isn't safe on the streets. What's this world coming to?"

"For some, the world might be coming to an end," I said.

"It ends for some people every day," said Shea. "But my world is still going good, real good. It isn't over any time soon. Like I said before, don't you have a jurisdiction problem here, Cape Cod wop cop? And if an ex-Statie gets in a jam, wouldn't the Staties be working on it? So why are you guys nosing around?"

"You know," I said, "sometimes a badge is like a big blanket. It can cover a wide area. Besides, maybe we're just here because we've missed the place and all the fine patrons. It's been awhile since I've seen the club."

"Well," said Shea, "maybe you should make it another four or five years before you come back." He laughed again and slapped the table in front of Sammy White.

Of all the people in the world, Tommy Shea is the one I'd like most to see leave the place, doesn't matter how. He was no good, pure and simple. What made it worse was that he had a family connection to the State House which gave him some cover. That was hard to bear.

I stared at Shea and then smiled. "It's been a nice visit. Give my respects to Joe Vito. Be seeing you, Shea."

Leo and I were silent as we walked back to his car. Once we got in, I asked Leo if I could bunk in at his place.

"No problem with that, Jack. Natalie will feel better about that, too."

"Yeah. You got any beer back at your place?"

Leo grinned at me.

"Good," I said.

"So Jack, what do you think Shea's going to make of this?"

"I think he's pissed that we connected him to Leary's getting jumped and that's just what I want. It puts a little pressure on him. He's more likely to make a mistake with some heat on."

"Aren't we getting beyond Agent Nelson's guidelines?"

"I guess, but we know Agent Watson's dirty, lazy or both. Agent Nelson doesn't believe it. So maybe we've got to bend the rules a bit to make him see what's really going on."

"You think Shea will suspect Agent Watson?"

"No reason to, but you never know. Sammy White's the real hair trigger there. Be a shame if he did suspect her. Of course, Agent Nelson might slap our wrists a little. Too bad."

"How do we explain this visit with Shea and White with respect to the Cape and Needham murders? We're just supposed to be looking for a connection."

94

"He doesn't know Leary was working for you. We've got the same story as White and Shea—Leary got mugged on the street, could be anybody who did it. They covered their tracks and ours at the same time."

Leo grinned. "Sometimes I think we're pretty good at this business."

"We are, old pal, we are, or I wouldn't still be here. Let's attack those beers."

Chapter Twenty-Four

I was on my second Scotch when Nat grabbed my arm. "Jack, take it easy on the drinks. There's plenty of time for you two to have a couple, but just a couple. I don't like to see you overdo it. You know what the doctor says about too much alcohol since your gut wound."

"Okay, hon, I'm all right. I can still handle the stuff."

Nat worried too much; sometimes the old bullet wound to my abdomen ached a bit. I had it under control, though.

It was Friday afternoon and I was waiting for Leo to arrive for the weekend. He showed up at my house just after four o'clock, as expected. Natalie escorted him to the backyard patio where I was stretched out in a chaise lounge, a drink on the table beside me and a radio playing a station I liked. They called the format *the music of your life,* with lots of Sinatra, Como, Deano, Tony Bennett, Nat Cole and big band swing; my kind of stuff. I had some beer in a cooler and a bottle of Dewar's on the table with some highball glasses. The sun had gone behind the clouds, but it was still warm enough for Bermuda shorts and a golf shirt. I wore sneakers without socks. Never could get used to sandals.

"You look like you're expecting company," he said as he went right to the cooler and popped open a cold beer.

"Take a seat, Leo. This is what living on the Cape is for; Friday afternoons sitting outside, some drinks, a few munchies and steaks on the grill. We are off duty."

"That's rich. When are you ever off duty?"

"Right now." I reached my glass out to Leo, whose beer bottle clinked against it. "May it last a while."

"Yeah. Tell Nat to take the phone off the hook."

"I heard that," said Natalie as she appeared carrying a tray of crackers with shrimp and cocktail sauce. "I thought you guys would be ready for these."

"Why don't you join us for a drink, hon?" I said.

"I'll second that motion," said Leo. "I'd much rather look at your pretty face than Jack's mug any day."

"Well, you know, since Jack's doing the cooking tonight, maybe I will. Pour me a Scotch-rocks, big boy."

Natalie swished her hips slightly as she sashayed over to a chair next to Leo. She still cut a great figure in tan clam diggers and a pink T-shirt. For a sweet Catholic girl, Nat could get a little brassy now and then, but not often. *Too bad she didn't show me this an hour ago.*

I dropped some ice cubes in a glass and poured in a shot for Nat and brought it to her. I moved back to my chair, grabbed my drink and hoisted my glass. "Once again, to weekends, good company and easy women."

"Let me know if you find any," laughed Nat.

"Me, too, Jack. I could use a break."

We all laughed and sipped our drinks, enjoying the moment. *May the mood stay with us this night.*

"You know, Leo, you ought to retire to the Cape, too," said Natalie. "Life is too short to spend it chasing bad guys all the time."

"So why is it that Jack, here, is still on the job?"

"Don't let this Manny Duarte case fool you," I said. "Most of the time, the pace here is a lot slower than with the METs. You ought to start making plans, old pal."

"Don't forget I've got an ex who has a great financial influence on my plans, which is why I started Barbado Investigations. I got to keep my head above water if I want to retire like this."

"Leo," said Natalie, "you and Jack could work as private detectives together right here. I'll bet there's enough work on the Cape to make it pay, but you wouldn't be knocking yourselves out. What do you think, Jack?"

"Wait. Let me get this straight. I'd be working for Leo?"

"*With* me, Jack. We'd be partners."

"I need another drink," I said.

"Now Jack, be careful. What if you get a late call again? Criminals don't care about your weekend, hon."

"Don't worry, dear. I've left word for Jim Pearson. He's on call tonight, not me. I am incommunicado."

"Okay then. But be careful just the same. I've seen you two party it up before." Natalie suppressed a giggle. She had seen Leo and me put down a few together over the years. It usually resulted in me sleeping somewhere other than in our bed, like on the floor beside the sofa. Leo often found the back seat of somebody's car, not necessarily his own. "Maybe you should get those steaks going, so you're not drinking on empty stomachs."

"Great idea, Jack," said Leo. "Medium rare with onions, please."

"Listen to him, would you? You'd think I'm running a r-r-ristorante here." I did my best at rolling the Rs.

"You are, pal. Welcome to Contino's Cantina."

"Hey, faccia brutto, you're mixing in some Spanish there. In Italian, a cantina means the wine cellar. The saloon idea comes from Mexico."

"It works for me. I'm not a purest with the language. Besides, it's got a good ring to it, don't you think?"

"Ah, what the hell. Nat, keep this guy out of trouble while I get the charcoal going."

I walked across the patio, drink in hand, and opened a bag of charcoal that was next to my kettle grill. I had already placed some newspaper and wood pieces in the kettle, which I lit. As the wood burned down to hot coals, I dropped the briquettes onto them, piling them up slowly.

"Haven't you heard, Jack? They've invented lighter fluid for that."

"I try to stay away from that stuff. It stinks and ruins the meat flavor. This is how my old man used to do it. Works great."

"Yeah, but it takes more time."

"That's fine with me. It just stretches out the cocktail time." I held up my glass again. *"Come stai, amico?"*

"Sto bene."

I went into the house to get the goods. I returned carrying a large platter with three steaks, onions wrapped in foil and some salt and pepper. I pushed the coals to both edges of the kettle, leaving the middle clear. The onions went on the grill first, directly over the coals. I then joined Leo and Natalie again.

"Got to let those onions cook a bit first. When we can smell them, it'll be time for the steaks. Leo, you need another beer?"

"Absolutely, Chief."

I popped open another bottle for Leo and checked on Natalie. "How are you doing, Hon?"

"I'm good, Jack. I'm taking it easy."

"That's cool, kiddo. Now, where was I? Oh, I was sitting here with a drink in my hand." I resumed my position next to Leo.

"Seriously, Leo, we could make a habit of this if you moved here. I know you can't do it right now, but maybe in a year or two?"

"Maybe, Jack. The idea is sounding better all the time. You really think we could make a go of it?"

"Well, there's not as much action as around Boston, but there are plenty of runaway teenagers and cheating spouses to keep a private investigator busy, especially if you market yourself right—you know, appeal to the deep pocket people. That includes the islands, too."

"Maybe we should test it out. You could run an ad in the yellow pages for Barbado Investigations."

"Hold on, folks. I'm still busy with the Dennis job. Let's not get ahead of ourselves."

I pushed my legs out straight and leaned back in my chair, savoring the aroma of the onions as it seeped out of the foil wrap. Then the phone rang.

Chapter Twenty-Five

I'd never expect a call from Tammy Watson, but leave it to her to ruin my Friday night. "How'd you get my home number?" I wasn't pleased.

"Agent Nelson gave it to me. I haven't got much time. I'm at a pay phone in Somerville and got to get back to Sammy's place. I called because I think I got something for you."

"Like what? It better be good."

"Sammy got real pissed off after your visit the other night. He doesn't like the fact that you're involved in the investigation about the ex-State cop. He figures there's something funny about that. Well, he got pretty drunk this afternoon while I was . . . with him at his place. He started getting mean. He wanted to hurt somebody and I was the only one around, so he started slapping me a bit. He'd mouth off about what he was going to do to you and Barbado and then he'd give me a backhand."

"Are you all right? Maybe you shouldn't go back there."

"Aw, I'm okay. I've put up with worse shit than that before. Anyway, he starts saying he's going to go to war with you. War, war, war, he says. Then he started rambling on about those creepy little war guys, how they're amateurs, but cheap help, so maybe he'll sick the war guys on you. He said Marshfield's not far from the Cape. I tried to get him to say more, because he wasn't making any sense to me."

I knew our visit to Shea and White would pay off. Maybe this was it. White was on the verge of doing something stupid, I was sure. Of course, once he sobered up, he'd have to make sure Tommy Shea was okay with it. I didn't want to get too deep into it with Watson. "Go on," I said.

"That's all I got out of him before he passed out. I figure that he's got some guys in Marshfield that he connects with for jobs, you know."

"Have you told Agent Nelson about this?"

"No, not yet, haven't had time. I called you because he was threatening you directly, so I figure you better watch your back. Of course, he may not remember much when he wakes up, but it's in his head to get to you. Maybe this bunch in Marshfield is what Agent Nelson is concerned about, maybe not, so I'll tell him soon. But this conversation with you never took place, okay?"

"Okay, Tammy, I understand. And thanks. Now you be careful with White."

"Don't tell me you're worried about me. That'd be a hoot."

"Yeah, one for the books," I said.

"Enjoy your weekend, Contino." She hung up.

I went back outside with Nat and Leo and picked up my drink, downed it, and then poured another before easing back down into my lounge chair. I guess my face showed something.

"Everything okay, pal?" asked Leo.

"That was Tammy Watson, of all the people to call me on a Friday night."

"No kidding. Jack, you underestimate your own charm."

"Who's Tammy Watson?" asked Natalie. "Don't tell me you're keeping a hot one on the side."

"Oh hon, I've got five or six of them, all good Catholic girls, too. This is an FBI agent and not one of my favorites, but she might be having a rough time with Sammy White after our visit with him and Shea."

Nat's face went grim. She knew I'd had this thing with Shea for years.

"White's been known to go ballistic with women now and then," said Leo. "I have no love lost for Watson either, but if she is getting on White's bad side, she could be in a rough way. He has a unique way of breaking off a relationship. So, why did she call you? Don't tell me she expects you to ride to her rescue."

"I don't think so. She told me to watch my back. She said White was ranting on about me being involved in Skip Leary's case."

"So maybe White and Shea know a lot more about that after all."

"And White might be about to do something stupid. He said he was going to war with me. Then he rambled on

101

about some war guys in Marshfield. Sounds like they've got some contractors there."

"Marshfield," said Leo. "Never heard of anything big coming out of that place, except maybe G. Lance Blakely, famous defense lawyer, flies his own plane out of the airport there."

"Me neither, but maybe we'd better check it out. I'll ring in with Jim Pearson on Monday, see if he's got anything in his old files."

I could feel Nat's eyes on me, so I gave her a glance. I knew the look. Her eyes darted to the Scotch bottle. I waved to her, letting her know I understood.

"Well, one thing's for sure," I said. "Sammy White is too blitzed tonight to do anything other than sleep it off. That's how Watson managed to get to a phone to call me. When he wakes up, old Tammy girl will know how to keep him distracted."

"She'd better keep his, ah, spirits up. It might be her best defense," said Leo.

I heard *Begin the Beguine* by Artie Shaw come on the radio and decided this was the right time to change the mood. I got up and walked over to Nat. She looked at me as I took her hand and helped her to her feet. I held her in my arms and we began to glide around the patio. "Who needs anything on the side when I've got this hot one right in front of me?" Nat looked up at me with a tight-lipped smile, her eyes getting just a bit moist.

Chapter Twenty-Six

The next Monday, I told Jim Pearson about my call from Tammy Watson and Sammy White's rant about going to war with me, and something about some guys from Marshfield. Nothing came to mind for him right away, but he said he'd check into it. It didn't take long.

By the time I'd finished my first cup of coffee, Jim called me over. He had a file folder in his hands. Before opening it, he pointed out his two large file cabinets against the back wall. He'd set up files years ago on every town in Massachusetts. He kept files on the other New England states, too, but not broken down by town . . . yet. He dropped notes and news clippings about crimes and criminal elements associated with each town. He held up the folder in his hands . . . MARSHFIELD. This guy was like having your own search engine.

"Your Marshfield folder looks pretty thin," I said.

"Yes, but that made it easy to go through. There are a couple of clips about a few drug crimes, an arson fire in '71, an assault on a police officer in '74 and this one. It really jumped out at me."

Jim pulled a newspaper clipping out of the folder and held it up for me. It had a headline that read, *WAR In Marshfield*. The date on it was 1976. "Well, now, isn't that interesting," I said. I took the paper from Jim.

"A couple of white kids decided they didn't like having a Black kid in the neighborhood, so one day they pounced on him at a convenience store. There was a local cop in the store at the time who broke it up and arrested the three of them for disturbing the peace. He took them into headquarters. He let the Black kid go, and the kid didn't want to press any charges. He called the parents of the other two, who had to come to the police station get them. Before they left, a local newspaper reporter showed up. Seems he heard the call on his scanner and made a story out of it. I guess the white kids saw opportunity in this and declared to the reporter that they were members of an organization called White American Resistance."

"How many more are in this organization?"

"Just the two of them, according to the article."

"There been anything since this?"

"Nope. Not that I've seen."

"I think I'm going to call on the Marshfield Police Chief. He just might have some trouble right under his nose. Thanks, Jim."

"No problem, boss. Let me know what you find out. I'll stick it in my file."

"That's a promise, Jimbo. That's a promise."

I poured myself another cup of coffee and looked up the number for the Marshfield PD.

There wasn't much traffic on Route 6, so the drive up to Marshfield only took about forty minutes. It was a warm, clear day with low humidity for a change.

Chief Bob Wiley was a big husky fellow, a bit shorter than me. He welcomed me into his office and offered me coffee, which I declined. He poured one for himself and eased himself down into a swivel chair behind his desk. I positioned myself in a soft chair facing him.

"What can I do for you, Detective Contino?"

"A couple of years ago some kids got a little news coverage in your town for attacking a Black kid in a store. It wasn't a big deal and the arresting officer decided to let the parents handle the discipline, so he let them go in the parents' custody. But a reporter heard about the fracas on his radio and decided to talk to the boys. They declared themselves to be part of an organization called WAR, White American Resistance. Do you know anything about it?"

"Yes, I'm afraid I do."

"So there's more than just two punk kids involved."

"Yes. It's a small group, but it's gotten larger over the last few years since that incident. They show up now and then at public gatherings, like a Fourth of July parade or a high school football game. They try to stir up trouble, but they haven't committed any crimes so far. It's just a matter of time."

"Why do you say that?"

104

"I took this job a little over a year ago. I had been working in a small town PD in western Maryland. That place was like being in the past. They had a big contingent of KKK there and sometimes they got nasty. One night a few of them got tanked up and happened to see a Black guy at a filling station. They took a baseball bat to the poor fellow, right there at the gas station. Killed him. Of course, we got them. Easy conviction because an out-of-towner who was there saw it and was willing to testify. There was plenty of hard evidence, too. The guy put up a fight and scratched one attacker's face. The one who owned the bat apparently couldn't part with his favorite Louisville Slugger and we found that in his car. It showed me that racism still exists in this country, so I decided to move back here where I still have some family. I didn't want to get too close to Boston, though. The bussing thing isn't very pretty, either. When I learned about the opening here, I jumped at it. I figured a nice seaside community would be quiet, a lot easier on the nerves. Know what I mean?"

"Yeah, Chief. I understand. Believe me." *The guy thinks like me.*

"So I have my men keep an eye out for these WAR guys. I figure they're going to bust out some day and try something to make a big splash. Why are you so interested in them, Detective?"

"I have reason to believe this WAR group, whoever they may be, *are* mixed up in bigger stuff. I can't go into detail on that just yet."

The Chief took a swallow of coffee and leaned forward, resting his arms on his desk. He tilted his head slightly to one side. "So is there anything you can tell me?"

I told the Chief about the Manny Duarte killing and the possible Needham connection and how an FBI undercover agent heard a target talk about some WAR guys in Marshfield doing a job for him.

The Chief sat back in his chair. "You know, Detective, I think I can help you out. Maybe you'll be helping me, too."

"That's how it's supposed to work, Chief."

"I want you to meet somebody," he said. He stepped out of the office for a minute and when he returned, he was accompanied by a good looking young officer, a Black female. "Detective, I want you to meet Officer Angela Green."

"My pleasure," I said as I rose.

The Chief pulled a chair into position beside me and motioned for the woman to sit down. She had a smooth, athletic gait. He went back to his chair and I sat down again.

"Officer Green has a background dealing with hate groups and she's keeping tabs on this WAR organization. Bring the Detective up to speed, Officer."

"Certainly," she said. "Before I was born, my grandfather was hung by a Klan group in Mississippi. They raided his cabin one night and pulled him out of bed. He had just bought a garage business a few months earlier and it was doing rather well. I guess those brave Klan boys didn't like the idea of a Black man being a success in their town, so they strung him up, right in front of my grandmother and my father, who was just a little boy. About a year later, after she scraped up enough money, my grandmother took my dad up north to Massachusetts, near Springfield. I grew up there, but went to college in Bridgewater. I liked being near the coast, so I settled here. I was going to be a teacher, but decided on law enforcement. I saw a program on TV years ago about Skinheads and Neo-Nazi groups, so I figured that if I was a police officer, I could work against the types of cowards who killed my grandfather. I've tried to learn as much as possible about those groups. When we heard about WAR right here in Marshfield, I told the Chief that I wanted to work against them in any way I could."

"So what have you learned about them?" I asked.

"Their racism is actually a type of class warfare. The Skinheads really started in England in the late fifties. Two groups evolved, one from the more affluent types and one from the blue collar people. They became known as the Mods and the Rockers and they got pretty violent toward each other. The Mods were well-dressed, wearing suits and long hair. The Rockers cut their hair real short and wore jeans with their cuffs rolled up and black leather boots and T-shirts. The Skinheads are derived from the Rockers and seem to dominate the groups in this country, but we've seen both types come and go from the WAR headquarters."

"You know where they operate from?"

Chief Wiley spoke. "There's a building back on Route 139. It's set back off the road a bit. That's where these WAR guys hang out."

"I'd like to see it."

"No problem. Officer Green, please do the honors."

"Yes, sir, Chief," she replied. "Detective, you might want to follow me in your car, since we'll be going back toward Route 3."

A few minutes later, we were on Route 139 about a mile from the exit for Route 3. Officer Green pulled into a small parking lot beside a diner and I pulled up beside her. She got out of her car and took the passenger seat in mine.

"See that dirt driveway across the street and that small corrugated building up there? That's it. That's where WAR hangs out. We keep an eye on the place, but they haven't done anything criminal yet."

"Not that you know of, Officer, at least not at that location."

"Well, they haven't committed any racial or hate crimes, just some minor noise at public gatherings, like I said. Chief Wiley said the Feds are interested. You think they've been doing bigger deals with whoever the Feds are looking at? Seems like strange bedfellows to me."

"Amazing how bigots can calm down when there's money to be made. Anyway, all I've got now is a hunch based on some info from an FBI undercover agent. If I can establish the connection, then this WAR bunch is going to get a lot of attention from the FBI."

"How are you going to make the connection?"

"Any way I can. First, I'll want to see who comes and goes out of there. I've got a guy who can do some surveillance for me, but I could sure use some help. He's part time. Used to work with me in Boston. Any chance you can put in some surveillance time, too?"

"It'll strain the Chief's budget some, but I think I can manage a few hours for you. Can't be indefinite, though."

"Understood. My guy's name is Leo Barbado. I'll have him coordinate with you. If we can watch this place for the next two weeks, keep track of all the cars going in and out, that'll be a big help. Pictures, too, if you can manage it."

"It can't be 'round the clock. I'm afraid I can only give you a few hours a day for those two weeks."

"I'll take whatever you can give me, Officer."

"Done. I'll wait to hear from Barbado."

"Thanks, Officer. Talk to you later."

Officer Green swung the passenger door open and eased her way out of my car, got back into hers and drove off. A good contact.

Chapter Twenty-Seven

Jared saw the beat up Chevy Nova in the Chicken Roost parking lot, its red-shirted driver sitting behind the wheel, staring blankly into the sky through the windshield. It was late in the afternoon and there weren't any customers in the bar, so Jared went out to see what red shirt wanted.

"Hey asshole, I told you to stay away from here. What do you want this time?"

"First of all, buddy boy, you don't *tell* me anything. Second, the message is same as before. Doc wants to see you pronto."

"Doesn't he own a telephone? Then I wouldn't have to see your ugly face."

"Doc likes to be careful about using the phone. Says it can cause trouble 'cause it leaves a record, ya know. He calls me, I call you; you call him. It all gets connected and cops have a way of finding this all out. So, just get your lousy ass up to see Doc tomorrow morning, understand?"

"What's he want this time?"

"You know better than that, buddy boy. You gotta talk to him about it. So cut the crap and do what he says. Now, go back inside and take care of business in your nice little gold mine of a place." Red shirt gazed at the Chicken Roost building. "Ya know, a guy could get interested in workin' a spot like this."

"Forget it. The owner's not selling."

"Maybe somebody can make him an offer he can't refuse." Red shirt broke out into a loud laugh that made a gurgling sound in his throat, like he was being strangled. The laugh stopped as quickly as it had started. "Tomorrow, go take care of business with Doc. Don't be late."

Jared stepped back from the Nova as red shirt started the engine. He peeled out and took off down the road. Jared stood watching in the parking lot, unaware that Will was peering out the window. Jared made a fist and slammed it against his leg. He knew he'd be getting a message from Doc. He just hadn't expected it so soon after their last meeting. And he really wished Doc would use another messenger.

Doc was waiting at his desk when Jared walked in the following morning. "I'll get right to the point, Mr. Wilkes. Our client may have a job for us on Cape Cod. He wouldn't make a commitment on it or go into exact details because he wants to be sure that we can handle it correctly and cleanly this time. The new recruit we used botched the last job. I trust you are better than he was."

Jared stood relaxed with his weight shifted onto one leg, his hands in his pockets. "I can handle it. I just need the right information."

"Well, you're going to have to prove yourself, to me and to the client. So I've got a little test job for you. If you handle this one to my satisfaction, then I can assure the client that we're ready for the next assignment."

"Like I said, I can handle it."

"Very well Mr. Wilkes, here it is." Doc handed Jared a manila envelope. Jared reached inside and pulled out the contents. There were three large black and white photographs of a female police officer, two showed her in uniform and one showed her on a lounger on a lawn outside of what appeared to be an apartment building. She was African-American. Another sheet of paper had a name and address on it, 10 Royal Crest Apartments, Route 139, Marshfield, MA.

Jared stared at the photos for a moment and then looked back at Doc.

"She's of no consequence to you, Mr. Wilkes, except for the fact that she is a Black female police officer, another example of how they are infiltrating our power structure and taking jobs away from hard working white people. She must be eliminated."

"When do you want it done?"

"Within the week. We've even gone to the trouble of finding out her work schedule. She'll be working the second shift for the rest of the week. You see, we've had our eye on her for a bit now. There's a boy in blue who's one of our boys. So she fits nicely into our plans. Be sure to destroy those photos when you're done. Any questions?"

"No."

"Good. Don't try to contact me when you're finished. I'll hear about it locally."

Jared nodded, put the photos and paper back into the envelope and left. The address was just down the street, back toward the highway. He headed in that direction, found the apartment complex and drove into the lot. Each of five buildings was clearly marked, using even numbers. Number ten was at the far end of the complex. There was a small parking area beside the building, with a chain link fence bordering the grounds, with forest beyond that. A Marshfield Police Department car sat in the lot. Jared felt a rush of excitement building in him as he swung his car around and headed out of the lot. In a minute, he was back on Route 3 southbound. He began working over scenarios in his mind of how he would carry out this job. A guy could get her as she came home from her shift. Or perhaps he could enter her apartment before she got home and be there waiting for her. What a surprise for her that would be. Either way, it would be one more achievement toward the mission and a notch on his belt. His energy was building, energy that he would soon turn toward DeeDee.

She was sunning herself on a blanket in the front yard when Jared drove up. She was on her belly, feet toward the road, wearing a blue bikini, the top unhooked. It was snug fitting and brief, just the way he liked it. Her skin was well tanned, but light, not a deep dark tan like Judy's. He saw her glance at him quickly and then turn back to a book in her hands. He hadn't spent last night with her, nor had he called her today. His eyes were fixed on her as he walked up onto the lawn, like a predator eyeing his prey.

"You must have had some big stuff going on last night. Is that why you didn't call?" She kept looking at the pages of the book.

"That's right," said Jared, as he got down beside her. I had something to deal with."

DeeDee turned her head toward him. "Couldn't you at least call, at least have the courtesy to let me know what you're doing?"

111

"Look, I'm sorry if it annoys you, but some things in my life don't involve you. It's not personal. I have some–well, business issues of my own that I have to take care of now and then. Can you understand that?"

"Okay, but you could have at least called to tell me you wouldn't be coming over."

He figured that if an apology would help her mood, he'd give her one. "You're right, Dee. I should have. I'm sorry."

He began to caress her bare leg, first with his index finger and then with his full hand. He ran it slowly from her knee up the back of her leg on the inside. It had the desired effect.

"I missed you last night," she said. "I hate it when I have to spend the night alone. I hate having an empty space in my bed."

"Gee, that poor bed must be real lonely right now, since nobody is in it. Why don't we do something about that situation right now?" His hand caressed her leg some more.

DeeDee let the book fall out of her hands. She turned toward Jared and stood up, not bothering to catch the bikini top as it fell off. He took her in his arms and kissed her and hooked his thumbs inside her bathing suit.

"Uh-uh, Mister. That part has to stay on until we get inside."

"Inside. Now there's a word with a lot of meaning."

DeeDee giggled and wrapped her arm around Jared's waist as they walked into the house. Jared spotted Judy reading a magazine in the living room as the couple came in. She looked surprised at the sight of the nearly naked DeeDee, who smiled at her as she and Jared turned toward the bedroom. Jared directed his glance at Judy.

Chapter Twenty-Eight

I got a call from Leo a few days after my visit with Chief Wiley in Marshfield. He had been doing the surveillance work on the WAR headquarters with Officer Green, and Skip Leary was helping him cover the hours as well as two additional Marshfield PD officers. He faxed me a list of cars and people seen coming and going with time of arrival and departure and descriptions. Pictures were on the way. I ran the plate numbers on all of them. Homerun.

A blue 1969 Opel Kadett, registered to one Jared Wilkes, was on the list. My dislike for Wilkes grew stronger after learning that he was connected to WAR. Extreme racism was in itself not necessarily a motive for murder, but knowing his reputation with the Boston Fire Department proved he could be moved to violence through his racist nature.

The list didn't show me anything that connected WAR to Tommy Shea. I wasn't ready to give up on that connection, though. I was sure they were linked after what Agent Watson had told me about Sammy White's ranting about WAR guys in Marshfield. I'd find the proof.

The thing that bothered me was that Wilkes had an ironclad alibi the night Manny Duarte was killed. He had been working at the Chicken Roost. His boss could attest to that and he left with Scott Seldon, one of his weekend pals. There had to be another piece to this puzzle. I went to the coffee pot and poured a cup.

"Jack, there's a call for you, Marshfield PD," said Jim Pearson.

"Got it." I went to my desk and put my coffee down before picking up the phone. "Detective Contino."

"Jack, it's Bob Wiley. Something terrible has happened and it might be connected to your investigation." His voice cracked. "Officer Green was murdered last night as she was about to report for duty. Her throat was cut as she was getting into her cruiser. One, possibly two guys jumped her. We're checking the footprints in the area. There's a cut in the chain link fence that borders the property. Looks like he came in through there, waited and then surprised her, too fast for her to fight back. No sign of the weapon yet. She was young, only on the force three years, and a good officer. Strange thing, though, her shield is gone. Looks like it was ripped off her shirt. The killer must have wanted a trophy."

The news hit me like a brick. "I'm real sorry, Chief. I know what this feels like, been there."

"Thanks, Jack. I want to get this guy real bad and if WAR is connected to it I want to destroy that bunch of punks, every last one of them. Looks like we're working together for sure now, Jack."

"Absolutely. Sounds like an amateur or a psycho. Pros don't do stuff like that. I'll need all the information you have, her personal record, family, friends that you know of, a picture."

"No problem. I'll have an officer run that stuff to you right away. Jack, me and my whole department want this guy."

I decided that Chief Wiley deserved to hear more information.

"Bob, I want to share something with you that I just found out about this morning. There's a guy here who's loosely involved with the Manny Duarte killing, name's Jared Wilkes. His girlfriend works at the place where Manny tended bar. It turns out that he dropped in on WAR headquarters the other day. His car was spotted by my associate, Leo Barbado. I have nothing solid to connect him to the Duarte killing, since he was tending bar when Manny was killed. But he's a racist asshole. He got bounced off the Boston Fire Department. Tried to stir up racist hatred among other firefighters and eventually picked a fight with a Black guy. That got him canned."

"Where is he now? Can you pick him up?"

"Easy, Chief. I'm going to go talk to him as soon as we're done. You say she was killed last night outside her apartment near eleven o'clock?"

"That's right. Jack, check this guy out and call me as soon as you can."

"You bet, Chief. Like I said, I'm real sorry about your loss. I'll talk to you later."

I couldn't finish my coffee. The taste had gone sour.

I took Jim Pearson with me to find Wilkes. *I might be dealing with a murderer, so it's good police procedure to have a backup.* It was too early for the young single crowd, but I figured the owner of the Chicken Roost would be awake. I was right.

Will Souther answered the door after two knocks. "Good morning, Detective and you, too, Officer. Must be something important for you to be out so early and with another officer, to boot."

"I need to see Wilkes. Is he here?"

"Well, Detective, you know young people today. Jared's got a room here, but he's got a girlfriend elsewhere. I suspect that's where he spent the night. I think she's . . ."

"I know the girl's address, thanks. Mr. Souther, was Wilkes working last night?"

"Yes, sir, his regular shift."

"When did he get off duty?"

"He knocked off at midnight, as usual, then he took a shower and left. I figured he was going to meet up with her someplace."

"Was he here the entire time of his shift?"

"Yep. It was a slow night, but Jared stayed right here. We just had a few customers in the bar, some I didn't know and two of our regulars—the Kenyon brothers, a couple of real estate men who like to finish up the day here. Jared likes to shoot the bull with them and they got a lot of bull to shoot." Will giggled like Walter Brennan in *Red River*.

"Okay. Thanks, Mr. Souther."

He nodded as we turned and got back in my car.

"Seems like Wilkes has a good alibi," said Jim.

"Seems so, again. It's hard to swallow, though. He's got to be involved in this somehow."

"You think the old guy's lying?"

"No, not likely, but there's something missing here. Whatever it is, it connects Wilkes to two murders. I'm sure of it. If he's connected to WAR and WAR is connected to Tommy Shea, I have even more reason to believe Wilkes is no good."

We got to the house rented by DeeDee O'Hare and Judy Black. I parked on the street. As we walked up to the door, I noticed a curtain move in a front window. One knock on the door and it opened. Judy Black stood there wearing a white T-shirt that barely covered whatever she had on under it, if anything.

"Good morning, Detective. What brings you here today?" Judy seemed to smile past me at Jim.

"We need to talk to Jared Wilkes. Is he here?"

"Yes, but he and DeeDee are still asleep, I believe."

"You're going to have to wake him, Miss Black. I need to speak with him now."

Judy's face went serious and she left the door open as she went down the hall and knocked on a bedroom door. Jim and I went inside and stood in the living room. Jim craned his neck a little to catch a look at Judy as she walked quickly down the hall. He looked at me and made a sound as if clearing his throat.

"Yeah," I said. "I remember what it's like to be that age, only I was married by then."

"I was single into my late twenties," said Jim.

"Be strong, Jimbo. Be strong."

He cleared his throat again.

Judy returned and said Wilkes would be right out. He emerged a minute later in cut-off jeans and a white shirt, the sleeves rolled up at the elbow. He didn't offer a greeting. Just as well. I wasn't in the mood for pleasantries from him.

"Where were you last night around eleven o'clock, Wilkes?"

"I was working at the Chicken Roost, as usual. You can check that out with Will, my boss." He paused for a moment. "Guess you've already done that."

"He backs you up."

"Why do you want to know?"

"A Marshfield police officer was murdered last night as she was about to go on duty."

"Gee, that's terrible. What's it got to do with me?"

Jim answered before I could speak. "You tell us, Wilkes."

"Testy disposition there, Officer. As you already know, I was occupied last night, at work and then here. I resent the implication."

My dislike for Wilkes was growing by the second. "What do you know about an organization called WAR, White American Resistance?"

The smirk left his face and he looked at the floor for a moment, as if contemplating his answer carefully. "I've heard of it."

"Just heard of it?" I said. "Have you ever been to their headquarters?"

He paused again. "I've been there. I know a guy, so, yeah, I've been there. Is that a crime?"

"No, Wilkes, but murder is. That police officer was a Black woman, as in African-American, a race that WAR professes to hate."

"A Black woman?" The voice was soft and came from down the hall. DeeDee O'Hare came into the living room, tying the waist strap to her short terrycloth robe.

"I told you to stay in the bedroom," said Wilkes.

"I want to know what's going on. Why are you badgering Jared?"

"Your boyfriend here is part of a group that hates Blacks, Jews, Catholics, Italians, Hispanics and probably the Easter Bunny. They're in Marshfield and that's where the police officer was killed last night."

"And you think Jared could have done something like that? Well, you're wrong. He was at work last night. You know that. And besides, Jared couldn't kill anybody. He's gentle and kind. Please leave. I don't want you here."

"Don't get excited, Miss O'Hare. We're leaving. Gentle and kind, huh? And I'm Santa Claus. Oh, one more question, Wilkes. Does the name Tommy Shea mean anything to you?"

"Not a thing," he answered, while turning toward DeeDee, wrapping an arm around her. I believed him on that one.

Back in the car, Jim stretched his arms out in front of himself. "Whoa, I can see why you don't like that guy. He comes across as somebody you can't stand right from the start. But he's got a tight alibi for last night. He seems to have his girlfriend locked up. Think she'd lie for him?"

"Probably, but it's his boss's word that matters here. He was at the Chicken Roost at the time of the murder."

"So he didn't handle the knife, but he might know who did. Or, he didn't have anything to do with this or the Manny Duarte killing. He's just a racist piece of crap the world can do without."

I hoped Jim's last idea was wrong. I'd hate to think that this bastard was not guilty of something. I needed to talk to Leo.

Chapter Twenty-Nine

"Screw them. Jared, I think you should sue those guys, or, something. How dare they come in here and accuse you of being involved in a murder, and in Marshfield."

"Calm down, Dee. They didn't really accuse me of anything. They just wanted to find out if I knew anything, and I don't. I was working last night, remember? They're pissed off that they can't figure out Manny Duarte's murder and they're getting desperate. So they go on a fishing expedition. This thing happens in Marshfield, and they think they've got a bite. They've got nothing. So let them go chase their tails."

"What is this WAR organization, Jared?" asked Judy.

"It's nothing." DeeDee answered before Jared could speak. "Jared told me about it a long time ago. Just a group of guys who want to keep this country from going to the dogs, that's all."

"Right," said Jared. "We meet now and then and talk about things."

""Like what?" asked Judy.

"Like school bussing, for example. There are some people, lots of them, who don't like what the politicians are doing to Boston. We look at who those politicians are and talk about how we can help people vote them out of office."

"So, you're interested in political action."

"Yeah, that's right. We want to change things, make sure whites are in charge, like it used to be. We work within the system."

"And I always thought you were just an easy going party kind of guy." Judy smiled out of the corner of her mouth.

"That's me, party guy. But there are parties and there are parties. WAR is like the beginning of a new political party, and it's growing all the time." Jared clenched his fists, his energy rising.

"Well, you know, I think it's pretty cool that you're willing to get involved in political change. We sure could use it. Scott doesn't even like to talk about politics or social change. Maybe I need to give him a nudge."

"Scott seems like a good guy. Maybe he just needs a chance to see things better. You should definitely talk to him sometime, find out what he thinks about things like who is supposed to be running this country, as the founding fathers intended. They were all slave owners, you know. That must have been a hell of a time. Imagine the economics of it alone. All the shit work, you know, like garbage pickup, factory work, stuff like that being done by workers who didn't have to be paid for it. And they wouldn't have a union to stick their noses into business owners' lives. You wouldn't have school bussing because those bastards wouldn't go to school. Think how much better your job would be . . . a school teacher who can focus on teaching and not having to deal with those little Black druggies." His voice grew higher, but not louder.

"Wow, you sure sound different, Jared, like you're really committed to this WAR thing," said Judy.

Jared didn't answer.

"Are there women in this party?"

"Sure. Well, not in our group right now, but women can take part. There's always a place for good chicks who know what's what. Are you a good chick, Judy?"

"You tell me, Jared." Judy grabbed the sides of her shirt and pulled it away from her body, then spun around, as if modeling. "What do you think, Dee? You liked Manny, didn't you?"

"Of course I did, most of the time." DeeDee's words were strained. "But, you know how those people can be as a group. I mean, they have their rights, too, but, well, Jared and his friends know more about this than I do. I'm . . . going to take my shower now."

"Oh, sure, hon. Go ahead. I'll have some coffee and check the TV news," said Jared.

Wilkes strode over to the TV and turned it on. When he turned back, Judy was still standing in the same spot, while DeeDee had left the room.

"I'd better get ready for my shower, too. Good thing there's another one outside." Judy turned her back to Jar-

120

ed and in a fluid motion, grabbed the bottom of her shirt and pulled it up over her head. She had nothing on under it. She dropped the shirt as she scampered down the hall and into her bedroom, closing the door.

Jared looked back toward DeeDee's room. She had gone into the bathroom and started running the water. He turned back, eyeing the T-shirt. He picked it up slowly, as if contemplating his next move, and then he strode down the hall to Judy's room. He stood outside, his hand over the knob, listening for movement inside. He heard none. Abruptly, he opened the door wide. Judy was standing across the room. She turned around quickly at the door opening and faced Jared, still naked, keeping her hands by her side.

"You forgot something." Jared didn't smile as he tossed the T-shirt at Judy and quickly shut the door.

In a minute, he was in the shower with DeeDee. "I thought you were watching the news," she said.

"Let's just say I've got my eyes on things." DeeDee wrapped her arms around Jared's neck and kissed him on the lips. Jared returned her kiss, eyes wide open.

Chapter Thirty

It was late in the afternoon when I got through to Leo at his office.

"I heard all about it," he said. "Real shame. The Marshfield guys doing the surveillance are pretty riled up. She was a good kid and they liked her a lot. She took any job and put up with some race crap from within the Marshfield PD. Not too much, I guess, just a couple of assholes."

"Got those everywhere, Leo. Might be one or two real bad ones up there."

"Afraid so. Too bad. The world would be better without them. So Wilkes has a tight alibi. Damn. Well, maybe he's just not involved in it. Maybe some other WAR jerks did it. We need some evidence to steer us in the right direction. Maybe Chief Wiley's got something by now."

"I'll give him a call. When can you get down to Marshfield for more surveillance?"

"I'll leave in about twenty minutes. Skip's been there all afternoon. We're building up a bigger list of cars and owners. Let's hope it gives us something."

"I'm going to contact Agent Nelson soon, too. I think he needs to know about this WAR group and Officer Green's death. I think this may be our connection to Needham. Talk to you later." *It's got to be the connection. It adds up.*

I called Chief Wiley first. He wasn't in, but the desk officer took my message. I decided to stick around the office, have a cup of coffee and call Natalie. The phone rang five times before she picked it up. "Hello."

"Hi, hon. Just wanted to tell you I might be a little late today."

"Oh, you're not going up into Boston again, are you?"

"No. I just have to stay around the office for a while. I'm expecting a call that I need to take. It's about a killing that took place last night in Marshfield. It may be connected to our investigation here."

"Oh, I heard about that on the news. That poor young woman officer. What a terrible thing. Isn't Leo working up there, checking on those awful racists you told me about? Tell him to be careful."

"I will, Nat. I will."

"Well, I'll cook a regular dinner and you'll have it when you get here. You be careful, too."

"Yep. Will do. See you tonight, hon." She was the constant in my life. No matter how a day went, going home to her made it better.

I went over to the coffee pot and poured a cup from what was left in the pot. It was strong, but that was okay. Late afternoon coffee from the bottom of the pot. What a treat.

I drank the cup half down and decided that in the interest of preserving my taste buds for dinner I'd had enough. After dumping the rest from my mug into the men's room sink, I took out a pack of gum from the middle drawer of my desk, slid a stick from it, peeled the wrapper off and fed it into my mouth. I crumbled the paper in both hands, sliding them back and forth before tossing the wad into the trash.

I walked over to a window and stared out. Life on the Cape was supposed to be easier than this. I'd spent a career chasing bad guys in Boston and the burbs, real bad guys. I took a bullet in a gunfight that left a fellow officer dead and a girl wounded. I took out the shooter, a guy who had murdered four hoods. On Nat's suggestion, I took this job in Dennis, said goodbye to Boston police work and moved here. I knew it wouldn't be crime free, but I didn't expect anything here to keep me involved with the likes of Tommy Shea or some racist boys club that might double as rippers for hire. Nonetheless, I wanted to get whoever was behind these killings: Manny Duarte, the guy in Needham and now Officer Green in Marshfield. People ask what life is about and get all jerked around trying to figure it out. To me, it was simple. Life is a big morality play and good has to beat evil. Simple to figure, hard to do.

The sound of a phone ringing and the desk officer's voice brought me back. "Chief Wiley for you, Jack."

123

"Got it." I hurried to my desk and picked up the call. "Yes, Chief."

"I wanted to let you know, Jack, that we found just one set of footprints in the dirt near the hole in the fence. Looks like a sneaker of some sort, about a size eight."

"Not a very big guy, then."

"No, I guess not. How big is this guy Wilkes?"

"Bigger than that. Worse, he's got an ironclad alibi. His boss says he was working the bar at that time and then he went over to his girlfriend's house and spent the night. The girl backs that up. Of course, she might lie for him, but his boss wouldn't. Got no reason to, as far as I can see."

"So Wilkes is clear?"

"Sure hate to admit it, but it looks that way. Still, he's connected to WAR, even admitted to going there sometimes."

"He did?"

"Yes, but he was clever. When I asked him about it, I think he wanted to deny knowing about them but he thought the better of it. A lie would have been a mistake. So he admitted to going there, but that doesn't make him guilty of anything. I'm not giving up on this guy, though. His girlfriend works where Manny Duarte worked. That's not much of a connection, but it is something. I got to just keep on him and find a slip up of some kind. Chief, I'm going to contact the FBI about WAR. We've got three murders that could all involve those guys, and the FBI is holding something in their hip pocket."

"You're losing me there, Jack."

"I'll explain it all to you later. Right now, I think I'll check out for the night, unless you've got something else."

"No, nothing else." I could hear the disappointment in his voice.

"Be sure to let me know when the service for Officer Green is. Leo and I will be there." I hung up the phone and wiped my hand across my face. I was tempted to call Agent Nelson right away, but decided against it. I was tired and pissed off. The sound of his voice probably wouldn't do much to cheer me up.

My mood improved as I pulled into the driveway at home and parked in my usual right side of the two car garage. Nat was in the living room reading a magazine. "I thought you expected to be late, but I decided to wait a while on dinner, just in case," she said.

"I got that phone call okay, so I decided to come on home. I'm glad you waited."

"I've got chicken ready for the grill and I'll make up a salad. How about some instant rice to go with that? It's an old family recipe."

We both smiled at the old joke, and I nodded. "I'll get the grill going. The first step in that process is a glass of bourbon, rocks. I'm on it."

Nat got out of her chair and came into the kitchen as I was about to fix my drink. She wore red Bermuda shorts that fit snuggly in the seat, and her legs were still smooth and tanned, with no sign of a vein. She was amazing. As she was walking past me I reached out with one arm and blocked her, sliding my arm around her and turning her toward me. She responded by wrapping her arms around my neck. I slid my arms around her waist and pressed her against me. "You know, having you to come home to makes my job a lot easier."

"I'll bet you say that to all your wives."

"Yep, every *one* of them."

I kissed her on the lips and held her tight, lifting her slightly off the ground. When I put her down, I hugged her and reached one hand down over her buttocks, squeezing gently.

"You know this kitchen is getting too small."

"What?"

"Every time we're in it together my ass keeps bumping into your hand."

"I guess I'd better shrink the rest of the house, then, cause that feels good to me."

"Me, too, big fella, me, too. What do you say you hold off on that drink? I don't want you to calm down just yet."

I scooped Nat up in my arms. "Let's go see how small the bedroom has gotten."

Chapter Thirty-One

The phone rang just as we finished dinner. I slid it off the wall cradle in the kitchen.

"Got some info about the vehicles outside WAR head-quarters," said Leo. "There's a red VW bug out there every day. Ran the plate and it belongs to one Wilfred H. Holiday, aka Doc. I guess that's after Wyatt Earp's buddy."

"Guess so. That all you got?"

"Oh no. You'll like this. Seems he did some time in county lockup a few years back in Plymouth for B and E, about ten years ago. And guess who his roommate was for about a month? It was none other than young Mr. Thomas Shea of Somerville who had assaulted a local police officer after a parking violation in downtown Plymouth. According to the warden, who used to be a screw back then, the two hit it off real well and became pals. They even sat together at meal time. Ain't that cute?"

"That's it, then," I said. "Shea definitely knows about WAR. We just got to prove it. That shouldn't be too hard, but then we've got to find out if they've been doing any business together. That's where Agent Nelson comes in. I'll bet my pension that's what he's been digging into. Time to see him again, buddy boy." I felt an energy rush.

"I hear you, Jack. It's not like I'm dying to see him again 'cause I miss his mug, but we got to do what we got to do."

"Okay," I said. "I'll contact his office and let them know we're coming."

We were in Agent Nelson's office at one-thirty the next afternoon. I told him about WAR, but not how I had heard about it from Tammy Watson. I told him that my man Jim Pearson came up with it from his files and we chased it down through the Marshfield PD Chief. Then the Marshfield officer was killed, her throat cut like Duarte and the guy in Needham. I told him about the WAR surveillance and how Leo connected Tommy Shea with this Doc guy.

"So I'm thinking that this connection is why you were holding us back, not to mention the Needham Police. Care to comment?"

"Maybe you should have just joined the Bureau, Jack, after leaving the METs. You're damned good at this work," said Nelson.

"Ahem." Leo cleared his throat.

"And I acknowledge your significant contribution in this, Barbado. Look, you guys know how hard it's been trying to bust up the Winter Hill gang. Believe it or not, with Shea running things, they got smarter and he's been able to dodge us every time. We had to move carefully. We knew about this WAR organization but not everyone could be told about it. I even had to keep Agent Watson in the dark for her own safety. When Shea moved up in the gang, we drew up a profile on him that included every place he did time and who his cellmates and buddies were. We learned about Doc Holiday and that he had some sort of neo-Nazi activities. When Davey Esteban came to us, he told us that Sammy White once talked to him about WAR, like it was an organization, and that it could do some jobs for him, but that he couldn't set the jobs up alone because of being dark-skinned and Italian. He told Esteban that Davey would really be on their shit list. I decided to keep a tight lid on this connection after the Needham killing aimed at Davey. Now, with this Marshfield officer being killed, I'm not sure what's going on. Why her? Is there a connection to the other two, other than maybe WAR just living up to their name?"

"Don't know. That's what we've got to find out. Either way, we've got to move. There may be other targets in WAR's cross hairs. Do you agree, then, that WAR is the connection between the Duarte killing and the Needham job, not to mention Marshfield?"

Agent Nelson folded his hands on his desk, his head down. He held that pose for a moment. "I guess it's a strong enough connection to let you pursue it, Jack."

"Okay, then. The MOs are all the same, basically, with the exception that Officer Green was outside her vehicle when she was attacked. We believe there's a South Shore racist group in bed with Tommy Shea and Sammy White. In order to solve the Duarte case, I need to talk to the Needham target, the guy Shea really wanted. I need to talk to Davey Esteban."

Come on, Nelson, get with me.

"As much as I hate to do this, Jack, I agree. But you've got to be very careful. We're keeping him under tight wraps. I'll set up a meeting for you. It'll be tomorrow."

"I'll bunk in at Leo's place tonight, so you can make it as early as you want. No point going back to the Cape tonight."

"I'll see what I can do about the time, but right now I can't promise a breakfast party."

"Understood."

"Boy, Jack, I bet your wife hates your Boston trips."

"You can bet on that. The only thing she wants me doing in Boston is seeing a Red Sox game, and I'm not too sure of that."

"I'll call you tonight at Barbado's place. I've got your number, Leo."

"I'm sure you do," said Leo. "You need anything, Jack?"

"No, I've got my goodie bag in the car. Let's get back to your place so I can call Nat."

I was getting anxious to solve the Duarte killing, but it was getting complicated. What started as a bizarre but isolated homicide in Dennis now had a much broader reach. One and possibly two other murders were connected to it. Worse, they probably involved the Winter Hill bastards and a creepy bunch in Marshfield. I hoped Davey Esteban could fill in some of the background for me.

Nat wasn't happy about me staying overnight off Cape again, but she was always prepared for it when I drove to Boston, so she wasn't surprised. "You know, I thought you'd be done with the FBI once you retired from the METs and we moved to Dennis," she said.

"I know, I know," I answered. "But the bad guys didn't know about my retirement plan, I should say *our* retirement plan. I'll be home tomorrow."

"Okay," she said and hung up. There was no "Take care of yourself," or "I love you, Jack." She just hung up. Boy, was I in the doghouse.

The call came from Agent Nelson around eight o'clock that night. The meeting with Esteban was set.

Leo wasn't invited. Since this was considered an interview, not an interrogation, Agent Nelson thought it best that I go alone. There'd be plenty of authority figures around Davey anyway, so no need to add another one. Leo took it in stride. I had a second cup of coffee, washed my breakfast dishes and set them in the drain next to the sink. At the appointed time, I got into my car and headed for the meeting.

After topping off my gas tank, I drove to the quiet rural town of Dover. Funny how such a bucolic setting could be so close to Boston, about fifteen miles west of the city. I drove through the center of town, which consisted of a pharmacy, a small food market, a gas station and a used furniture store. A half mile out of town was the address I was given. A left turn took me down a narrow, wooded road. The road went up a short hill, and a large white clapboard house with an attached barn to its rear was on my left. It was my destination.

There was a circular driveway in the front and a parking area to the left of the house beside the barn. I pulled onto the property, going past a post with a sign on it reading "K. L. Knowlton, Surgery." There were three cars already in the small lot, all backed in to their spaces. I saw more parking room to the left behind a row of pines, so I parked there. According to my instructions, I went up to a side door flanked by tall, wide windows, next to the parking lot. The door opened before I could get my hand on the knob. A tall FBI agent in a suit greeted me as I went through the door which led into a large kitchen, lined with white wooden cabinets on the walls. The stove and fridge were white, as well. Two other agents in plain clothes stood against opposite walls. A young man with dark skin sat at the rectangular table in the middle of the room. He held his head down.

"Detective Contino, come in," said the suit. "I'm Agent Delock."

"Nice place. Where's the doctor?"

"As you might guess, there is no doctor," said Delock. "This is a safe house for the Bureau. The surgeon's residence and home office make good cover. We can have four or five cars here and it looks normal. The circular drive makes it easy to get in and out quickly."

"Cool," I said.

"Yeah, well, enough of that. Here's your man, Davey Esteban. Say hello to Detective Contino, Davey."

Davey looked up, with caution. "Hello."

Agent Delock motioned to the other agents. One went out into the parking lot, closing the door behind him. The other went out a back door that must have led to the barn. Agent Delock remained behind. "There's fresh coffee on the counter, Detective, some doughnuts in that box and milk in the fridge. Help yourself."

Delock walked around the room, drummed his fingers on the counter and left through another door, closing it.

Davey was in a chair at one end of the table. I took a seat in the corner next to him.

"Hi, Davey. I'm Detective Jack Contino from the Dennis Police. Did they tell you why I'm here?"

"Just that you were coming and I needed to cooperate with you."

"There was a murder in my town recently and it looks exactly like the one in Needham that was supposed to be you. I think they're related, but in order to prove that, I need to know everything I can about what happened to you and why they wanted you dead. I know you've been through this before, Davey, but please help me here. I need you to tell it all again, to me."

"I guess that's all right. It'll be like practicing my testimony. Could I have a glass of water first?"

"I'll get it for you, Davey." I found a glass in an upper cupboard and poured some cold water from the kitchen sink. Nat sure would love a big kitchen like this. I put the glass down in front of Davey as I reclaimed my seat. Davey took it and lifted the glass to his lips, sipping some water.

"You know I like to go to the race track on my nights off," he said. "I like the trotters over in Foxboro. Only I wasn't having much luck lately. This was just over a year ago. One night, I was losing real bad, so bad I started cursing out loud. I guess I had a few beers by then, too, so that didn't help. Then a guy dressed real nice comes up to me and offers to help me out. He says he'll loan me some money, so I can make back the money I lost."

"Who was this man, Davey?"

"He said he was Salvatore DiFino. He was a business-man. He said he knew I could make the money back, so he loaned me a few bucks right out of his pocket. I kept losing, though, but Mr. DiFino, he said he wasn't worried. One night, he made me fill out an application for credit, said it was just a routine business deal."

"What sort of questions were on that application, Davey?"

"Just the usual stuff like on a job application, you know; my name, address, where I worked, stuff like that. But I didn't put down my address on account I was staying with a friend for a while until I could get my own place. I didn't want to get somebody else involved, you know?"

I nodded. It sounded like Davey knew in his heart that there was something wrong here, but he did it anyway. His compulsion for gambling was strong. "Go on, Davey."

"Well, I kept losing. Hah. What else? But Mr. DiFino said it was okay. Then I started winning again. Of course, he was right there at the window with me when I collected. He took most of the money back toward my debt, but he'd leave me enough to keep on betting. Then I'd lose some more. Even though I'd win some and pay back Mr. DiFino, I was losing more than winning. I was sinking, man."

This was a strong connection. Salvatore DiFino, aka Sammy White, best pal to Tommy Shea. He had many pursuits, and loan sharking was one of them.

DiFino liked creating his own collection methods, which included breaking people's bones, cutting off a finger or toe, beating someone senseless or even killing them. But Shea taught DiFino that there were better ways.

I was pretty sure I knew where this story was going but I had to hear it all.

Davey took another sip of water, grabbed a deep breath and continued, "I was getting in deeper and deeper and was afraid I'd never get ahead. But Mr. DiFino said I could work off my debt by doing odd jobs for him. I had no idea what he meant, but I found out. There were other people who owed him money, so I had to go see these people and make them pay back. Mr. DiFino took me around to some of these places, you know, in Boston and Somerville and Medford and other places, and he introduced me as the guy they would see each week. At one place, a small store in Boston

131

on Charles Street, Mr. DiFino didn't like the guy's attitude because the guy said he wasn't going to pay him anymore. So Mr. DiFino broke the guy's finger on the counter. He smacked it with a jar that was right there. At another place, it was an older woman who got a little feisty, you know, and he slapped her right across the face, knocked her down, with her mouth bleeding. Geez, that was really bad, but I couldn't do anything. Mr. DiFino said this was the way to make sure people who owed him money paid him back. I got the message."

"Davey, most of those people, the shop owners for example, they didn't owe him money. He was collecting protection money. DiFino would protect these people from DiFino. If they didn't pay him, he'd hurt them even worse. It's called extortion, and it's a serious crime. You're going to help those people by testifying against DiFino and Shea."

"Who's Shea, Detective?"

"Tommy Shea. DiFino works for him. You never heard of him?"

"Nope."

"Be honest with me here, Davey. DiFino never mentioned Tommy Shea to you?"

"No, never, honest."

"That's okay, Davey. Don't worry about it. You're doing just fine."

Damn. I hoped Davey's testimony would lead to an indictment against Shea, but I'll have to keep digging for that one.

"That extortion thing, Mr. DiFino said I was into that. He said I could go to jail, so I'd better do as he said. He was the only one who could keep me from getting arrested. But one time I said I just couldn't do this anymore. Mr. DiFino laughed and then got real mad. He slapped me around pretty good and hit me hard in the gut a lot. He said I'd just made a mistake and that everybody makes a mistake now and then. So now I would come to my senses and not make any more mistakes. That's when he got me into delivering drugs."

I sat for a moment just looking at Davey Esteban. What a sad case. If he didn't have bad luck, he'd have no luck at all. Lots of people have gambling problems, but they don't get mixed up in the Mob, usually.

Sammy White was a predator. He went looking for poor souls who he could take advantage of and eventually profit from their misfortune, or whatever you want to call it. I know he learned that from Tommy Shea. White didn't have the smarts to think of that technique by himself. Shea was slippery. He sure could cover his tracks.

"Go on, Davey. What happened next?"

"I got to the point where I just couldn't take it anymore. I was doing stuff I hated doing, you know. I was afraid to go to the police. I don't trust the cops. No offense, sir, but I guess you're not a regular cop."

"I'll take that as a compliment."

"One night I was watching TV and it had an FBI guy in the story and it made me think maybe that's who I should call. So, I looked up the FBI in the phone book and got the Boston office. I met Agent Nelson. I told him all this and he said Mr. DiFino works for some big shot in the Mob, but he didn't say who it was. Maybe that's this Shea guy you mentioned. Anyway, he said I should just go about my business and they would make sure nothing happened to me. The next night when I was at work, there was a woman working there. She was new. Do you think the FBI put her there? Wow, I didn't know women were in the FBI."

"Just go on, Davey."

"About a week later, I was feeling kind of sick one night, so I asked Rocco, my boss, if I could go home early. He said fine, so I did. Then that night, this other guy gets knifed right there in the lot. I feel awful about that. Agent Nelson says it was supposed to be me. I don't understand it. I thought I was with Mr. DiFino."

"He knew you had talked to the FBI, Davey."

"But how? Was he watching me all the time?"

"Yeah, I guess so." I couldn't tell Davey what I really thought. The picture was now very clear to me. Agent Nelson sent the wrong person to do undercover work at Rocco's. Agent Tammy Watson was too close to Sammy White. He knew she was an FBI agent. Why would she suddenly have an assignment at Rocco's where Davey worked? That was good luck for White. It was a clear tip off that Davey was talking to the Feds. Now I was convinced that she was dirty, on the take from Shea and White. She was in bed with White in more ways than one. Agent Nelson insisted that

133

wasn't true and he continued to support her, but that was going to end. She was responsible for the death of Richard Allenson in the attempt on Davey. I was going to prove that once and for all, somehow.

That was all Davey had to give me. I saw no need to start telling him about WAR and how I believed they were used as a contractor to kill him. After all, he was here to talk to me, not the other way around.

"Davey, I want to thank you for doing this today. You've got a lot of guts. I promise you that you'll be fine. DiFino and his pals are never going to hurt you again. Once you've testified against DiFino, the FBI will put you in a witness protection program. It might be a little strange at first, but you'll be alive and safe. You'll get your life back. They'll explain it all to you when the time is right."

"I sure hope so, Detective. It's all been pretty scary. I guess I'd better be careful about taking loans from people at the track."

"Davey, those days are over for you. Don't ever go back."

"Yeah, I guess you're right." Davey looked down at the table and then took another drink of water. He looked more alone than anybody I'd ever seen.

Chapter Thirty-Two

While Jack was meeting Davey Esteban, another meeting was taking place at the FBI office of Agent Nelson. Tammy Watson had decided it was time to let Nelson know about Sammy White's ranting about guys in Marshfield. There might be an attempt on Jack Contino's life and Nelson should know about it.

Sitting across from Nelson's desk, Agent Watson told her story. Nelson sat quietly as she went on about Sammy White's threat against Jack Contino. Nelson's stoic posture didn't bother her, for it was the norm with him. Then he spoke and the mood in the room changed.

"Agent Watson, it's time to let you know that we already know about the organization called WAR. We believe that they've served as a contractor for gang killings, but haven't got the proof yet to act on them."

"You what?" she asked, sitting up and leaning forward. "You already know about them? Just when were you going to tell me this?"

"Calm down, Agent. We couldn't tell you because it might have put your life in danger."

"Hey, don't give me that crap. I put my life in danger as part of the job." Watson stood up and faced Agent Nelson. "Shea and White aren't Mr. Nice Guy and his brother. I'm used to sticking my neck out, but I do it because I know what's going on here—whether or not the Bureau has my back. I know Sammy White pretty well, and know how to handle him when he gets nasty. Let's just say I know how to give him happy thoughts. But if I ever thought you were holding back on me . . . then I'd have no back up and wouldn't know how or when to move, what direction to take when dealing with these guys."

"I made the decision to protect you, whether you like it or not," said Nelson. "As long as you didn't have that information you couldn't make a slip of the tongue that might get you killed. Believe me, Agent Watson, I honestly believed that it was the right decision, and I still do."

"So I work all this time just to find out what you already know. That's just great."

"No, Agent Watson, that's not why you've been working undercover. I said we know about the organization called WAR. But I also said that we have no proof. Your job is to get that proof. We have to make a solid link between WAR and Tommy Shea's gang. We have to learn about specific contracts. That's why I let Jack Contino in on the investigation. His case in Dennis and the one in Needham are too similar to be a coincidence. And I'd rather have Contino and Barbado working on this quietly than to have the Needham PD bumping into the Bureau and the State Police. Too much noise could send Shea and WAR heading for cover. Contino is talking to Davey Esteban today to learn what he can before Davey testifies in court. Of course, that's pending an arrest, which we can't make yet. So you see, Agent, this has gotten very complicated. In fact, I might as well tell you, there's been a third killing with similarities to the others. A Black female police officer in Marshfield was killed, her throat cut from behind."

Agent Watson sat down, her lips drawn tight. Her eyes began scanning the room, as if looking for words.

"You have to be very careful, Agent, but we need you to dig further. Tommy Shea did time in Plymouth ten years ago with a guy named Holiday, who is the head of WAR."

Agent Watson stared at Nelson.

"Three people have been killed in the same way, and one of them was supposed be Davey Esteban, because he was talking to us about Sammy White. We can't arrest anybody on Davey's testimony alone. We need more proof. We want to get Shea and White once and for all, but we have to destroy WAR, too. You, Agent Watson, have to help us get that proof."

Agent Watson didn't speak for a moment. This job had started out as a big adventure, getting in tight with Mob guys, even taking one as a lover. Sammy White's power as a Mob man and his physical strength made him very appealing to her. She knew he was a killer, but she never worried about that. She finally realized the enormity of the mission she was on.

"I guess I'd better get back to work, then," she said, rising from her chair. "I wonder who they'll get next, me or Contino? Ah, just joking, boss."

Agent Nelson nodded. He understood her need to stay loose, but he had to stress the importance of her mission and the potential danger. "Jokes have their place, Agent. That's good. Just don't forget how important this mission is. The Winter Hill boys have to be stopped, but they're just a gang out for themselves. WAR is another matter. That group breeds hatred toward anybody not like themselves. We can't let organizations like that thrive in this country. We don't need little Hitlers running loose here. I don't think even Shea knows what he's dealing with. Being in league with the likes of WAR and their hate mongers is like sitting on nitroglycerin. Be very careful."

"I got it, boss. I plan to get the job done and get out of this in one piece. Maybe I'll write a book about it one day."

Chapter Thirty-Three

Jared awoke beside DeeDee, who was lying face-down. She had kicked off the covers completely. She was a beautiful and tempting sight, completely naked with statuesque curves. Her butt was tight and compact, and he felt a twinge of excitement. He had to pee real bad, though, so the temptation to mount her again had to wait. He grabbed a bath towel, flung it over his shoulder and walked into the bathroom across the hall. When he returned, DeeDee had curled up into the fetal position and pulled the top sheet over herself. He noticed the clock on the night table and remembered he had a business appointment. He had to take care of that before going to work, so he took his shower solo for a change and got dressed, leaving without waking DeeDee.

Jared drove west along Route 28 into South Yarmouth. Crossing the Bass River Bridge, he turned right into the parking lot of an old clapboard-sided motel building, peeling white paint. The Bold Pirate Motel featured a tall statue of a peg-legged sea robber, sporting a black patch over one eye, an effective symbol—if not original. He pulled his car into a parking space at the far end of the lot.

He walked up to the last unit at the back of the motel. A stereo was playing *Light My Fire* by The Doors and the smell of pot and stale beer filled the air. He almost walked right in, but then decided knocking might be safer.

"It's Wilkes," he said, rapping his knuckles on the door twice.

There was a delay before an answer came. "Come in, come in. I've been waiting for you."

Jared pushed the door open and saw his business associate sitting on the bed wearing faded blue jeans torn at both knees. He was barefoot and bare-chested, with a two-day beard and uncombed brownish hair down to his shoulders.

Sidney L. Fish was in his late forties, a short, thin, pot-smoking drunk with a record of B&Es and petty thefts, who entertained himself often at local watering holes, including the Chicken Roost. Jared had met him two years before while working at the Hotel Belmont. It was way out of Sidney L. Fish's league, so the manager told Jared to throw him out. Fish was already half smashed, so Jared had no trouble handling the guy. Knowing a loser when he saw one, Jared figured Fish might come in handy one day if he ever needed a slob to do some dirty work for him and maybe take the fall if things went bad. He'd slipped Fish a ten spot and gotten his address.

Jared soon learned that Mr. Fish had a temper and could be a nasty fellow when sober. On a spring night some months after meeting him, Jared took Fish out for drinks as a way of cultivating his favor. Before they finished their first round, a tipsy patron bumped into Fish on his way to the men's room and spilled some of Fish's drink. The guy wanted to fight.

The participants moved outside and Jared went along, interested in how Fish would do. A couple of customers joined in to watch. The drunk tried a couple of swings, right hand leads that Fish ducked easily. When he swung again, Fish hit him hard on the chin, knocking him back. After a few more hits, the guy was about done, but he thought a broken beer bottle on the ground nearby was his chance at salvation. By the time the guy had it in his hand, Sidney L. Fish had produced a switchblade from his coat pocket, slashed the hand holding the bottle and grabbed the guy by the scruff of the neck, bringing the knife point up to his throat. The scared drunk dropped the bottle and begged for mercy and Fish sent him on his way. Jared took Fish back inside and bought him all the drinks he could handle.

"Hi, ho, Jared. I been thinking about you. Got something for me, do you?"

Jared reached into his pants pocket and pulled out an envelope bulging with bills. "Five hundred big ones for you, Sidney. You did the job well."

"Well, the next time it's going to cost you double. Five hundred for icing a cop is pretty cheap."

"You seemed happy with my terms when I told you about it. Maybe there are other talented people out there who are, shall we say, down on their luck like you."

"Hey, I didn't mean I'm not happy with the five. I really need it." Sidney caressed the cash. "This will help me keep a roof over my head and a bag or two of good weed in the drawer. I just think I proved I can do the job and a raise would be nice if you have another one."

Jared walked across the room to a window that looked out to the parking lot and showed a limited view of the Bass River. "Well, Mr. Fish, a raise isn't out of the question and I just might have such a job soon, but if it comes down, you'll have to be sober."

"Not a problem, boss man. I cut down to a six pack a day for this Marshfield job and just a little weed. Of course, no weed on the job, but nothing wrong with a little trip out after, you know. It was a shame to have to waste that Black chick. What a sweet little body under those cop clothes. Managed a quick feel as I slit her throat. Would've been fun to have some time with her, but a target's a target, I guess."

"And don't ever forget that. You celebrate after the job, not on it. That cash ought to get you laid."

"Yeah, boss." Fish picked up a beer bottle and swigged some. Room temperature beer didn't seem to bother him.

"Take it slow, Fish. I might be calling on you soon."

"You know where to find me, Wilkes."

Chapter Thirty-Four

Sidney L. Fish couldn't take it slow with a bunch of cash in his pocket. Shortly after Jared paid him off, he hopped into his old Ford Fairlane and made his way to a favorite saloon of his—the Sand Dune in West Dennis, near the beach.

Fish parked his car and slipped into the establishment by way of a side entrance leading directly to the bar. That door would be locked after six, but Fish beat it by a couple of hours. The bartender saw Fish enter and shook his head. George had been working here for years and recognized Fish as a regular customer. Fish was in a bragging mood about making a big score.

"Give me a shot of bourbon and a Bud. Yes, sir, bourbon and a Bud, bourbon and a Bud."

George hesitated. When Fish produced a wad of cash from his pocket, George went ahead with his order. "You been working, Sidney?"

"Yep, old man. Got the cash to prove it." Sidney grabbed the bourbon and shot it down, following it with his beer chaser.

George stood there with both hands on his hips. "I probably don't want to know what kind of work you've been doing."

"No, sir, you do not." He slid the shot glass back toward George. "Hit me again, my friend."

"I'll run a tab for you, Sidney." George poured him a second shot.

"You know me, Georgie, I'm not afraid of honest work. Of course, I'm not afraid of a little dishonest work, either. Ah hah." He made short work of the bourbon and again followed it with beer. He pushed the glass back to George and smiled without speaking. George obeyed.

After six shots and more beer chasing it down, Sidney L. Fish got pretty talkative. There were only two other patrons in the bar at the time, so George leaned on his forearms at the bar in front of Sidney, got comfortable and listened to his tale.

"You know what, Georgie, I got talent. Yep, that's right. These punks running around here these days, they got nothing."

"What kind of talent have you got, Sidney?" George was amused.

"I got a way of making people disappear. Gone. Presto. Never to be seen again."

"So you're some kind of magician I guess."

"That's right, Georgie. And here's my magic wand." Sidney pulled his switchblade from a pants pocket and pushed the button. It made a metallic cracking sound as it opened with startling force over the bar. George jumped back.

"Whoa, Sidney. Put that thing away." George looked around to see if anybody had seen what Sidney had done. The other patrons tried to look casual, but after a minute they were paying their tabs and leaving.

"Now see what you've done, Sidney. You're driving my customers away."

"Aw, don't worry about them. Little scaredy cats. There'll be other folks soon enough. Like I said, this is my magic wand. It makes people disappear." Fish ran his finger over the side of the blade, then closed it up and put it back in his pocket.

"Sidney, you're just kidding, right?"

"I wouldn't kid you about my talent, Georgie, my new-found talent. You see, I was always good with a blade, but I never had to make nobody disappear before. Then I meet this guy, just call him J.W. He says he can get jobs for me, so he does. He lets me know what he wants done, you know, who, and he gives me some . . . guidelines, and I do the job and he pays me real good."

George felt a shiver run down his spine. "You're good at telling stories, too, Sidney. Real good."

"Yep, that too. But my real talent is making people disappear, like that little Black chick up in Marshfield, that cop. A quick slash across her throat and presto, she disappeared from the planet. Oh, I didn't hide her or nothing.

142

They got her bloody little body. It's a figure of speech, my man, a figure of speech. Presto, disappeared." Sidney made an attempt at snapping his fingers. "My first big job for . . . J.W. Got five hundred for it. Mighty nice."

George wanted to shoot down some whiskey himself. Instead, he poured another one for Fish. "Here, Sidney, this one's on the house."

"Well, you're a gentleman and a scholar, Georgie boy."

"Yeah. Hold down the fort, Sidney. I got to take a leak."

† † † †

George went into a back room and gasped for breath. A few deep ones helped him calm down. Was Sidney for real? Was he just making this up? George remembered something about a Marshfield cop in the news. No, Sidney was small time. He must be bullshitting. George went into the kitchen, grabbed a small glass of water and drank it down.

When George reappeared in the bar Sidney was gone. A fifty dollar bill was pinned down under his beer bottle. George hustled out the side door, but there was no sign of Sidney. Just as well that he left. George had some thinking to do.

Chapter Thirty-Five

I was finishing my morning coffee when Jim Pearson came into my office looking too serious for such an early hour.

"Jack, there's a guy out front who you need to talk to. It might be a lead in the Angela Green murder."

I pushed my coffee mug aside and motioned to Jim to bring him in. Starting off a day with good news would be a switch. Jim motioned to the guy from my door threshold.

"Thank you," he said to Jim, as he squeezed past Pearson and into my office. "Hello, Detective. I'm George Rogers. I tend bar at the Sand Dune in West Dennis."

"Yes, I've seen you there. My wife and I go there once in a while. Nice place and it caters to an older crowd, which is more to our liking at this stage."

"I recognize you, too, Detective. I knew you were a cop, a police officer. We've just never been introduced."

"What's up, George? I understand you've got something about the Angela Green killing. Is that right?"

"Angela Green? Is that her name, the cop in Marshfield?"

"Yes, George. What can you tell me?"

Jim Pearson remained standing just inside the office door. I wanted another set of ears to hear whatever George had to say. He told us the entire tale of Sidney Fish's bragging the day before at his bar. Fish could just be a full-of-it drunk, but something in the story caught my attention.

"You said he referred to his boss as J.W. Am I correct?"

"Yes, that's what he called him. He said, "Let's call him J.W., or something like that, like he didn't want to say the guy's name. Is that important?"

"So he had a lot to drink and then left while you were in the back room."

"Yes."

"Do you know where Sidney Fish lives?"

"I believe he said he stays at the Bold Pirate motel on Bass River."

"Okay, is there anything else?"

"No, that's it, Detective. Look, Sidney always seemed harmless to me. I know he's a petty thief and he's done some jail time. At least, that's what he likes to say, like that makes him a big man or something. He's usually kind of fun to have in the bar sometimes, but this story chilled my bones. And the way he handled that knife, it was like he became another person when he had it out. I don't want to get the guy in trouble if he was just slinging it, you know."

"I know, George, but you did the right thing. We'll have a talk with Mr. Fish and clear this up."

"Say, you won't have to mention my name, will you?"

"No, we'll try to keep you out of it. But, you understand that if Fish is involved in that killing, you will have to testify."

George looked down and rubbed his hands. "Gee, I hadn't thought of that. Okay, I guess I can handle it."

"Don't worry about a thing, George. We'll handle this from here. It's probably just a drunk getting a little loud. Thanks for coming in. Oh, say, what kind of car does he drive?"

"I think it's a Ford Fairlane, dark red, I think."

George left quickly without saying another word. He looked pale as he went out.

Pearson walked toward my desk. "What do you think, Jack?"

I stood with my hands on my hips and took a breath. "I think we'd better go over to the Bold Pirate. George said Fish talked about a guy with the initials J.W. Could be Jared Wilkes. Hiring another guy to do his dirty work would explain how he managed a tight alibi. We know he's in with WAR. Maybe killing a Black Marshfield cop was a big move for them. They screwed up on Davey Esteban, so maybe this was a way of getting back in good graces with Tommy Shea and company."

"Shall we get some back up?"

"Yes, in an unmarked car. We don't want Fish panicking at the sight of a cruiser. But hold on for now. I want to get a search warrant and notify the Yarmouth PD. He's in their jurisdiction. We'll need them. This might take a little while."

Chapter Thirty-Six

I pulled into the parking lot at the Bold Pirate motel, followed by another unmarked car with two of our uniformed officers inside, and one from Yarmouth. I let Jim Pearson out at the motel office to identify us and confirm that Sidney L. Fish was a tenant. He was gone for only a minute. "Number fifty at the end."

I drove slowly across the lot and spotted the old red Ford outside unit number fifty. I motioned to the uniforms to park away from the Ford while I pulled up beside it. The uniforms covered the back, in case Mr. Fish tried to exit through a rear window. Pearson, Sergeant Wilson from Yarmouth and I went to the front door. I knocked hard. At first, there was no answer. I knocked again and still no answer. I looked at Pearson and tried again. Nothing. I began to draw my revolver. Wilson and Jim did the same. Then the door began to open and we slid our weapons back into their holsters.

A ruffled-looking man in wrinkled clothes; brown slacks, brown socks and an open white shirt, stood in the door. "Jesus Christ, I was trying to sleep. Who the hell are you guys? What do you want?" He rubbed the graying stubble on his face repeatedly.

"I'm Detective Jack Contino with the Dennis Police. This is Sergeant Wilson from the Yarmouth PD and Sergeant Jim Pearson from Dennis. Are you Sidney Fish?"

"That's right. I'm Fish. What'd I do, run a red light or something?"

"We'd like to ask you a few questions, Mr. Fish. May we step inside?"

Fish stood in the doorway trying to shade his eyes from the daylight. "Hell, no, you may not step inside, not without a warrant."

"Well, what a lucky day for us. I just happen to have one right here." I pulled the folded warrant out of my coat pocket with one hand and pushed Fish back into the room with the other.

The unit was an efficiency, about twelve by fifteen, with a queen bed, a kitchenette and a table for two against the wall. There were empty beer bottles on the table and the remains of a pint of bourbon. Sidney must have tied one on the night before, and the room smelled like it. There was an ashtray on the table, too, with a funny looking cigarette. Strike one for Fish.

"Take a seat on the bed, Sidney," I said.

"Hey, who do you think you are?"

"I said, take a seat." I pushed Fish down onto the bed.

Jim Pearson started searching the place, starting with the kitchenette. He took out a plastic bag from his pocket and put the funny cigarette inside. Then he opened the cabinet under the sink and crouched down to look deep inside, using his small flashlight.

"I have some questions for you, Mr. Fish."

"Oh, yeah? Like what?"

"Like what do you know about the murder of a Marshfield police officer named Angela Green?"

Fish rubbed his hand across his face. "I . . . I don't know anything about a murder."

"That's not what you said last night."

"Last night?" Fish shook his head, as if trying to remember. "Last night. I guess I don't remember much. Hey, can I get a drink of water?"

"Go ahead, but stay cool, pal. Don't try anything cute." I put my hand on top of my gun. "Jim, let him get some water."

Fish went over to the sink after retrieving his highball glass from the table. He rinsed it out a couple of times and filled it with tap water. He guzzled it and then filled it again, making short work of the second glass. Dehydration the morning after isn't much fun.

"Now get back on the bed, Sidney."

Jim Pearson stood up, ready for a foolish move from Fish. Fish didn't try anything, just did as I told him.

"Jim, find anything interesting?"

"Yes, indeed. He's got four plastic bags in this cabinet, each one pretty full with pot, if I trust my nose. Got to be over a pound. There's also a bunch of papers here, too, and, oh look at this in the back." Jim's arm extended into the cabinet and he pulled out a small scale.

Jim continued searching the kitchenette, opening a wall cabinet. He took out an empty soft drink bottle with perforated tinfoil covering the top. There were some cotton balls and a brown medicine bottle with some fluid in it, all the paraphernalia used for freebasing cocaine. A plastic bag with a hefty amount of the powdery substance was tucked in the back.

"Either Mr. Fish has a hobby or he sells this stuff," said Jim.

"This is very bad, Sidney. This looks like a violation of the narcotics act, possession with intent to sell or distribute. You know what, Sidney? I think we're just going to have to take you in and finish our talk at headquarters. You're looking at two and a half to ten, provided this is your first." Sidney didn't make a sound as I handcuffed him and called for the uniforms. "Read him his rights, boys. We can't forget to do that. We don't want this lowlife taking a walk."

Jim and I remained behind to finish our search. While Pearson finished up in the kitchenette, I went over to a dresser and opened the top drawer. Sitting right on top of some clothing, off to the left, was what we were looking for, a switchblade knife, the blade retracted. I wrapped a handkerchief around it and pushed the button to release the blade. I looked it over, then retracted the blade and put it in my coat side pocket. "The knife looks clean, but the lab can check it for any blood residue."

I looked around the rest of the room and found a small ledger book with names, dates and amounts of product written in it. There was also wad of bills, six fifties, in the top drawer. I showed the wad to Pearson. "That's a lot of cash for a drifter like Fish. He's probably got more in his pockets and doesn't even know it. That would back up the possible sale of pot. But being all fifties, I'm thinking it could be what's left of a good payoff from J.W."

"Looks pretty bad for Mr. Fish," said Jim.

"I hope so, because if he's the guy who killed Officer Green, we can use that to get at Wilkes. Bad day for J.W., too. Let's go. We got what we were looking for and more."

Chapter Thirty-Seven

When we got back to headquarters, I called Leo to tell him the news. I told him to contact Agent Nelson and bring him along to the Cape. We had to print Fish anyway, so we could let him stew for a while in a cell and let him sober up before the party.

I felt obligated to call Chief Wiley in Marshfield. I needed to work on Fish before making any moves on WAR, but the Chief had lost an officer. If the shoe was on the other foot, I'd want him to call me.

"Hello, Chief," I said. "I have some news for you and a big favor to ask. I'll start with the news."

"I'm listening, Jack. Go ahead."

"We have a lead in the Officer Green case. It might be very big or it might be just a drunk blowing off some steam, but I don't think so." I told him about Sidney L. Fish and his blabbering recently at a bar and how the bartender came to see me about it.

"You think this is the killer?"

"I do, Chief, but we need to interrogate him further. We're holding him on possession of drugs with intent to sell. I'm hoping to use that as a way of getting him to work with us. I think he was put up to the job on Officer Green by Jared Wilkes, but we got to tighten that up."

"That's the guy you liked for the hit on Officer Green in the first place, but he had an alibi."

"Right. Hiring another hit man would explain how he got such a tight alibi. But, as of right now, Fish hasn't fingered Wilkes. He just gave the initials J.W. to the bartender he blabbed to."

"I want to come down and see this guy, Fish."

"Okay, Chief, but here is where the big favor comes in."

"I hear you, Jack. What do you need?"

"I need you to let me handle this guy my way. Don't rush into an arrest. Besides, we don't have enough evidence yet."

"Jack, I want to get this guy. If he's Officer Green's killer, I want him real bad."

"I know, Chief. Believe me, so do I. The first time we talked, I said there was more to WAR than meets the eye. I drew you a vague picture involving the FBI. When you get here, I'll give you those details."

"Then I'd better get on my horse and head your way."

"Leo Barbado and our FBI contact are also on the way. When everybody gets here, Fish should be more presentable and sober, I hope. Whatever we get from him has got to be good for court."

"I understand, Jack. It's hard to keep cool in this situation, but I'll manage."

"Good. See you soon, Chief."

I had another call to make right away, this time to the District Attorney's office to get the okay to make a deal with Fish. I explained the situation, including the FBI involvement. No problem. I met with the DA shortly after coming to Dennis because I wanted to cover that base early. I had done it many times when I worked with the METs. Working with potential snitches was actually simple most of the time. If they were the type that couldn't handle hard time, they usually were pretty anxious to do what you wanted in exchange for a break. You had to square it with the prosecutor, though. I had a pretty good track record in Boston and the Barnstable County DA knew about it, so this call was rather routine.

I could imagine how anxious Chief Wiley was to get here. We'd both left more troubling jurisdictions for jobs in southeastern Massachusetts, where we could kick back a little and add some years to our lives. These cases were blowing that all apart for both of us. I wondered if he had a wife like Nat, strong understanding, always there. Probably. It's hard to survive in this business without that kind of support. Maybe Nat and I would meet her someday, kindred spirits and all that stuff. It's real good stuff.

Chapter Thirty-Eight

Chief Wiley got to Dennis well ahead of Leo and Nelson, so I decided it would be the best time to fill him in completely. We got some coffee and sat down in my office and I told him about the FBI's interest in WAR and their possible connection to the Winter Hill gang.

"So that's who the Feds are looking at. You think WAR has done some hits for Shea and his boys."

"We think they tried to do a hit in Needham last fall, but they got the wrong guy. The real target is now in Federal custody for protection. We have no idea who the hit man was, but it might involve Jared Wilkes. If WAR screwed that one up, the Angela Green killing might have been a way of making up for it, proving that they still could be counted on for other jobs."

"But why hire Fish to do the job for him?"

"My guess is that he wanted to insulate himself. That's a good idea, but it was bad execution. Wilkes isn't nearly as smart as he thinks he is. He hired Fish as his insulation, but he's a loser, too. He must have seen Fish on a good day and never saw the whole package. Fish has a big mouth and a great liking for booze and drugs. He's not somebody you can rely on for dangerous work. If I'm right, then Fish can help us nail Wilkes. Once we've got Wilkes, we can go right up the chain to the big boys."

"Are you sure that will work?"

"The FBI has an undercover agent named Tammy Watson. If she gets the evidence we need from the inside, it should dovetail with what we get from Fish, Wilkes and so forth."

"It sounds like a big gamble, Jack."

"It is, like everything in this business. But we've got to go for it. Tommy Shea's the head man at Winter Hill. He's as rotten as can be, and his reach extends a long way. He's hurt a lot of people, and he's deep into a lot of illegal business. The FBI wants to shut him down real badly and so do I. I've been anxious to see him put away for a long time."

"I understand that, Jack, but I'll be happy just to get Angela Green's killer. Everything after that will be gravy for me."

"Understood. Here's how I want to play it. Fish doesn't remember what he told that bartender about killing Officer Green. We don't have any hard evidence against him, but I'll bet we can scare him into thinking we do—and we've got him hard on the drug dealing. If he's a previous offender, he's looking at five to fifteen. We'll tell him we'll cut him a break if he'll give us Wilkes for Officer Green's killing. I'm betting that Wilkes will turn on Fish, so we'll get him there as well. Then we play a similar game with Wilkes to get WAR and WAR leads us to Shea."

Leo popped his head in my office door, Agent Nelson behind him. They were in casual clothes, as per my instructions.

"The plan sounds simple enough, Jack. Hope you're right."

The men made greetings, and I put down my coffee. "Time for a change of scenery. Let's see how Mr. Sidney L. Fish is doing."

The Dennis PD had an addition to the back of the building constructed recently. I was able to convince the Chief that one of the things necessary to good police work is an interrogation room, complete with an observation area separated by a two-way mirror. Fish was taken there after getting sober, cleaned up and given a nice orange jumpsuit. I went in alone while Chief Wiley, Leo and Nelson went into the observation area.

Fish sat at a table in the middle of the room, facing the two way mirror. He looked at me as I came through the door to his right, then looked down at the table, trying to avoid the mirror. I sat in a chair opposite Fish.

"We've got some things to talk about, Sidney. You're in a whole bunch of trouble."

Sidney squirmed in his chair and spoke softly. "Any chance of getting something to eat around here? I'm getting hungry."

154

"Don't be thinking about food, Sidney. You've got more important things to worry about. There'll be food a little later. Be thinking more about doing up to ten years for possession with intent to sell, fifteen years if we find you've got a prior conviction."

"Fifteen. Hey, shouldn't I have a lawyer in here?"

"The Public Defender will be along shortly. You can be sure of that. So you don't have to talk about the drug charges right now. I've got a more interesting subject for you, the murder of Officer Green in Marshfield."

"I told you I don't know anything about that."

"Oh, but I think you do, Sidney. You blabbed about it to a local bartender and that's very bad for you."

"I must've been drunk and just showing off, that's all, just blowing off steam."

"Now why would you do that, Sidney? Why claim to do a murder just to impress a bartender and scare a few patrons? There are all kinds of things you could have bragged about. Why a murder?"

"That's just his word against mine. I was just talking big, that's all. You arresting me on that, too? Nobody's going to believe it. It was just the booze talking, that's all."

"Well, Sidney, how did the booze know she was slashed across the throat?"

"I read it in the papers. It was all over the news."

"No, Sidney. You're wrong. That was kept out of the papers. It was too gruesome for her family to hear, so they just said she was killed with a knife, but it happened just like you said. Her throat was slashed."

Sidney's face was drawn tight and he began to fidget in his chair.

"You're bullshitting me. I tell you I read about it."

"What paper did you read, Sidney?"

"I don't remember."

"Well, I can show you back copies of the Boston papers and the Cape Cod Times. You won't find any mention of her throat being cut, Sidney."

Fish sat back in his chair, looking side-to-side, as if searching for an escape route.

"Don't you have any air conditioning in here? It's getting kind of hot, for chrissakes."

155

"There's something else you need to know, Sidney. We found your knife, a nifty little switchblade. I know you think you cleaned it off, but there's a pretty new game in town for police. It's called Match the DNA."

"The what? What the hell is that?"

"It's found in the blood, Sidney. DNA. It's like finger-prints, only in the blood. It's unique to each person. And the lab scientists only need a microscopic amount to check it out. So if there's just a small amount of blood residue on your knife, they can check it out for a DNA match with Officer Green. Then it's bye-bye Sidney, life without parole. What do you think, Fish, are they going to find some of her blood on your knife?"

Sidney grew more agitated. He seemed to be hyperventilating. I thought he was going to throw up.

"Relax, Sidney. I believe I can help you out."

His breathing slowed and he looked at me. His mouth opened, but he couldn't speak. There was a pitcher of water and some paper cups on the table, so I poured him some. He gulped it down.

"Okay, Sidney, here's how it's going to go. I'm going to help you and you're going to help me."

Sidney wiped his mouth with the back of his hand. He drank some more water. "What do you mean?"

"Here's what I think, Sidney. I think you got in way over your head and you're going to pay a steep price for doing somebody else's dirty work. J.W. is a guy named Jared Wilkes, isn't it?"

Sidney looked as if I'd picked his pocket.

"Don't try to be cute, Sidney. If you want my help you got to play straight with me from here on out."

"Yeah, yeah, it's Jared Wilkes. That's right."

I stopped him right there.

"Remember, Sidney, we haven't arrested you for Officer Green's murder. But it's looking pretty bad for you, unless you help me out. We think Jared Wilkes was sent to kill Officer Green by a racist group called White American Resistance, WAR. He hired you to insulate himself, so he actually didn't have to do the killing. We think he and his buddies at WAR are messed up with some very bad people, but we need more evidence to prove it. That's where you can help me."

156

"But I . . ."

"Stop. Sidney, if you agree to help us get the evidence we need, we can make sure you don't spend the rest of your life in prison. In fact, you may not have to go to prison at all. You might just be given a new identity and sent off to Never-Never Land. So, here's the deal. We're going to let you walk out of here. We're going to drop the drug charges, for now, and you're going to go out a free man, sort of. You're going to get in touch with Wilkes and get him to talk to you about why he hired you to kill Officer Green. Get him to admit that it was WAR and who in WAR gave him the job. Be careful about it, but be fast. We need this as soon as possible. Oh, and you'll be wearing a wire with a small tape recorder. Sergeant Pearson will show you how it works."

"How the hell am I going to do that? I don't know, Detective, I really don't know."

"Just be calm, Sidney. Go back to your place and relax awhile. I'll give you cab fare. You know where he works?"

"Yes, I do."

"Then go there this afternoon and see what you can find out. Don't press too hard. Just try to get him to open up. When he does, dig a little deeper. Tell him you want more jobs, that you two make a good team, et cetera, et cetera. And remember to turn on the recorder."

"Okay. I get it."

"Call me tonight from your place when you've got something, anything. Call me twice a day after that. Sidney, this is very important, so listen carefully. We're going to have officers watching you constantly. You'll be on a very tight leash, so don't get any ideas about getting away. You'll have three police departments and the FBI following you day and night. Don't even think about making a cute move, or we'll be all over you. Get it?"

Fish nodded. I led him out of the room and Jim Pearson took him from there, got him back into his street clothes, showed him how to operate the wire and sent him on his way. I met Leo and Chief Wiley back in my office.

Agent Nelson looked agitated as he spoke. "I don't feel comfortable letting Fish walk out the door, Jack. I hope you know what you're doing."

"That's why you and Leo are going casual. Fish doesn't know either of you, so you two are going to go check into his motel. His room's already wired for sound with a transmitter. You just keep a little receiver/tape recorder tuned in to hear whatever he's doing. When he goes to see Wilkes, follow him there and go in separately. We'll also have some officers in an unmarked car following him everywhere. He's not getting away. I'll call off the Public Defender. Hop to it, boys."

"I don't suppose you want me to go along with them, Jack?" said Chief Wiley.

"Naw. Three's a crowd, Chief. I know this is hard for you, but you should go back to Marshfield and wait to hear from me or Agent Nelson."

If things went as I hoped, we'd be tightening the noose around all of those bastards: Wilkes, WAR, Sammy White and Tommy Shea. If they didn't, a big mess could get a lot messier.

Chapter Thirty-Nine

Tammy Watson never wore a wire to record anything Sammy White or his associates might say in her presence. There was too great a chance White could find it. After all, he couldn't keep his hands off her. Her body parts were all fair game for White, and she liked it that way, too. Whatever she heard and passed on to the Bureau was dependent on her memory, not Memorex.

She wore a dark blue miniskirt, a white sleeveless pullover top and open-toed black pumps when she drove to Russo's Restaurant in Dedham on Route 1. Sammy White frequented the place because his cousin Mike, a retired light heavyweight boxer, owned it and they served great food. Sammy liked the gnocchi best and Tammy loved it, too, having never heard of it before coming here. She parked in the lot across the street and went inside.

White was sitting at the bar waiting with a glass of red wine. Tammy walked up to him with that smooth, sexy rhythm to her walk that always caught the eyes of most men and a few women, too. White threw his free arm around her, placing his hand firmly on her butt, pulling her toward him. She put an arm around his shoulders and kissed him firmly on the lips.

"About time you got here, doll. I was getting lonely."

"You mean horny, don't you?"

"Well, that, too, babe." He patted her ass twice and then the motion turned into a caress.

"Sometimes, the way you feel me up I think you're really looking for a wire."

White laughed a low growling kind of laugh and drank from his wine. "Let's go to our table, babe. Go ahead over. I'll get you a glass. Hey, Joey, another Chianti." The bartender stopped wiping glasses and complied with the order. He knew Sammy.

Tammy eased herself into a chair at their table for two near a window, just outside the kitchen. She smiled when Sammy eyed her well-exposed legs as he walked to the table. A waiter was right behind Sammy. The waiter took the order from White and left just as cousin Mike appeared.

"Hey, Mikey, good to see you." Sammy got up and the two hugged, patting each other on the back.

"Good to see you, too, Sal."

"You know, babe, this here guy was almost middle-weight champ. You always should have fought middle, Mikey. I never knew why you went up to light heavy."

"Ah, doesn't matter now, Sal. I had a good career either way."

"You sure did. This kid fought all over the world, babe. What a world traveler. My money was always on you, Mikey. You were a money maker."

Tammy was used to this talk, so she smiled and nodded and drank her wine. She took hers slowly while Sammy gulped his down and ordered another. By the time dinner arrived, he was on his fourth.

"You know, sweet cheeks," said Sammy. "Something's been bothering me."

"Why, Mr. Cool, what could possibly be bothering you?"

"You remember Friday last week, we had some afternoon fun, you and me at my place. I talked to you about some things maybe I shouldn't talk about, business things. We had a few drinks, did our thing and then fell asleep."

"You mean passed out, don't you?"

"Whatever. You must remember what I talked about, don't you?"

"I know you were pissed at that Detective Contino. I guess you don't like him."

"He's a goddamned son-of-a-bitch, and someday I'm going to get his ass."

"Yeah, that's pretty much what you were talking about."

"What else? Do you remember?"

"No, that's it. You were pissed off at Contino and wanted to get him someday."

Sammy looked at Tammy. He took another drink of wine. She wondered how much he could remember.

"I seem to remember waking up after a while and you weren't there."

Tammy knew he was testing her. He wondered if she'd have the balls to lie about that.

"You were out like a light. Well, you know I have to check in now and then with my supervisor, otherwise he might get suspicious, or even worried about me. Ain't that rich? So I went out for some air and made a call to the Bureau to check in. Just routine stuff, Sammy sweetie. Are you sure you were up, or are you just remembering dreaming all this?"

"No, it's no dream. So you admit that you went out."

"Yeah, like I said, I had to check in, that's all. Then it was back here to be with my sleeping beauty. I wanted to play again but you were way out. I couldn't . . . rouse you up at all, and I tried."

Sammy showed a slight smile. "Too bad I missed it. Tonight is a good time to make up for lost opportunities. Follow me back to my place and we'll see what we can do."

Sammy got up first and helped Tammy out of her chair. He dropped a bunch of money on the table without ever calling the waiter, more than enough there to cover everything.

When they got back to Sammy's house in Somerville, they went into the living room where Sammy had a wet bar with a single stool. Tammy sat on the stool and Sammy went behind the bar. He produced two wine glasses and a bottle of Chianti which he opened.

"You know what I'd like, babe?"

"Well, I can imagine."

"I'd like to watch you get naked. No bump and grind stuff, you know, just take your clothes off, and don't hurry."

Tammy nodded and stood up. She was used to Sammy's games. She moved away from the bar stool and kicked off her shoes. She unzipped the skirt and slid it down over her hips and let it fall to the floor. Next, she raised her top over her head and peeled it off.

"Careful, Sammy, your eyes are going to fall out of your head."

He didn't smile. White took a sip of wine without moving his gaze away from Tammy as she unhooked her bra and lifted it off her breasts, dropping it at her feet. She made a three-quarter turn before pushing her panties down and

161

stepping out of them. She shrugged her shoulders, as if relieved of the burden of clothing and looked over at Sammy.

Sammy White eyed her steadily. Tammy noticed how he looked at each of her garments as she took them off, like an inspection was taking place. She passed.

Sammy made a motion with his index finger for Tammy to come over to the bar. She gave him a full frontal view walking back to her wine glass.

"Why don't you join me, Big Boy?"

"I will soon enough. Right now, just indulge me a bit. I like being fully dressed while in the company of a beautiful naked lady. I'll put on some music."

In a moment, the voice of Tony Bennett came softly from the stereo, singing *I Left My Heart in San Francisco*. "An oldie but goodie," said Sammy. Tammy accepted him as he slid his arm around her, easing her away from the bar. He held her in a dance posture, but they swayed back and forth, more than danced. Her body felt warm and soft against him, and she felt him become aroused. It was as close as he ever got to creating a romantic moment. Tammy nudged herself in as close to him as she could. He responded by wrapping both arms around her and sliding his hands over her buttocks, then up and down her sides. She sensed this was different from all the other times.

Chapter Forty

Leo watched Agent Nelson pace the floor awhile in the room at the Bold Pirate motel. It was just after two o'clock and they had been there for a couple of hours. Nelson stopped pacing and sat down at the table holding the large tape recorder and small speaker attached to the receiver that was catching every sound from Sidney Fish's room. He adjusted the control knobs, stopped, then adjusted them again.

Leo lay back on a bed with his head propped up by two pillows. He held a bottle of cola in his hands and sipped from it occasionally. "Tell me, Agent Nelson, what do you think you'll do when you retire?"

"What? When I retire? I really haven't thought about it much, not at all in fact. It's still a few years off for me."

"What? You're no spring chicken. How far off can it be?"

"As far off as a mortgage and two kids in college make it. Retirement isn't on my radar screen yet."

"Jack says I should start thinking about it now. He says he wishes he'd given more thought to it when he was with the METs, but it's like you say, when you've got others to worry about it's hard to plan for yourself. He and Nat are okay, though, so they're not hurting or anything. But he's still working."

"You mean he needs the cash? I thought he just couldn't give it up."

"I think it's a little bit of both. The Dennis PD job is a lot slower than the METs and it acts like a transition period to real retirement. The extra cash flow is helping him feather his nest for old age. He says I should do the same. Maybe you should, too."

"Yeah, old cops never die. They just retire to Cape Cod and let their slacks out at the waist."

"Hey, that's not bad, Agent Nelson, not bad at all. I'll have to remember that. Maybe I could have . . ."

Leo stopped talking when he heard the sound of a car pulling up and parking in front of Sidney Fish's room. He motioned to Agent Nelson to turn up the speaker. In a few seconds the driver was in Fish's room.

"Hello, Jared. Isn't this a surprise? I was going to come over to your place later."

"Nice to see you, too, Sidney. Did you get laid yet?"

"Oh, I've been fucked. Real good, too."

"Glad to hear it, Sidney. Always happy to hear when a man's getting some action. But enough of the pleasantries. I've got some business to talk to you about."

"I'm all ears, Jared."

"Remember I told you that I might have another job for you pretty soon? Well, this is pretty soon. My employer gave me another assignment and I need your skills to help me take care of it."

"Okay. What's up?"

"There's a local cop that needs to go. His name is Jack Contino and he's a detective in the Dennis PD. It's got to be done this week. Here's a picture and some information about him, like his home address, his car, et cetera."

Agent Nelson looked at Leo. Their expressions went cold. They heard the sound of papers rustling.

"Shit, not another cop. Hey, this is getting risky. And a detective, too."

"Don't worry, Sid. You'll be getting more cash for this one. That Marshfield cop was small time. This is going to pay much better."

"Ah, the Marshfield cop, you mean that Black woman?"

"Yeah, Sidney. Who else would I mean? How many Marshfield cops have been wasted lately?"

"Well, yeah, I know. It's just, well I'm a little rattled by all this, so sudden . . . and a detective."

"If you're not up to it, Sidney, just say so."

"No, no. I can handle it. Hey, hey, hey, this is going to be cool."

"That's more like it, Sidney."

"Hey, ah, Jared, this employer of yours, anybody I know?"

"That's not your concern, Sidney."

"I know, I know, but since this is looking big time, I just wondered, you know. Hey, there's some good Scotch over on the counter, there. Want one? Pour me a glass, too."

"Don't mind if I do."

Leo and Agent Nelson listened to the sound of glasses clinking together.

"Listen, Sidney. Have you ever noticed that there are a lot more Black bastards taking over this country? Well my employer is going to take care of that. We're just getting started, too. You see, there's this organization in Marshfield. They're all over, really. It's called the White American Resistance, WAR. That's why we took out that little Black bitch of a cop."

"But Contino is white?"

"He's a wop, Sidney, a Catholic wop. They're almost as bad. The kikes, too, and the spics. WAR is going to give this country back to the whites, where it belongs."

"Yeah, baby. I'm with you."

Once again glasses clinked.

"Okay, Sidney. There it is. Here's five hundred up front. You can use your knife if you want to, but he's going to be a whole lot tougher than the little bitch. I can get you a gun if you want."

"No, no, I like my knife. He'll never see me coming, so don't worry."

"I'll know when it's done because it'll be big news. I'll see you shortly after that. You might need a vacation somewhere when you're done, just to be safe. You'll be able to afford it."

"Okay, got you on that. No problem."

"Nice seeing you, Sidney. Keep up the good work."

Agent Nelson stood up with his hand on his face. "Holy shit. Jack's going to love this one."

"I'm already loving it," said Leo. He took a deep breath. "This gives us Wilkes, WAR and Fish for Officer Green's murder."

"Yes, but it doesn't give us Shea. We've still got some work to do. I hope Agent Watson comes through on that."

"Oh, yeah, Agent Watson."

"Knock off the sarcasm, Barbado. She's got her neck stuck way out on this."

"Yeah, I guess I should give her a break. Even Jack seems to be changing his mind about her. So what do you hear from her lately?"

Agent Nelson didn't answer the question. "Let's give Fish a visit and a ride back to the police station. He's probably breathing a bit heavy right now."

They identified themselves to Sidney Fish and put him in the car. As they were driving, Leo repeated himself to Agent Nelson. "You didn't answer my question a minute ago."

"What question was that?"

"The one about Agent Watson. What have you heard from her?"

"I'm waiting for her to check in. I don't want to move on WAR until she does."

"Can't you reach her first? Things are getting hot."

"You know we can't do that. I don't want to blow her cover. She'll have to check in when it's safe."

Chapter Forty-One

Jared sat in the living room at DeeDee's place reading the newspaper and working on a cold beer, when Judy walked in the front door carrying a shopping bag. Her tight blue denim cut-offs seemed shorter than usual, and her white T-shirt was tucked in at the waist, accenting her bosom.

"Hi, Jared. My, it seems awfully quiet around here. Where's Dee?"

"She went to the mall for a while. She said her mother's birthday is next week and she wanted to get her a present. She'll be gone for some time, I'm sure."

Judy walked past Jared, giving him a glance and then putting her bag on the kitchen table. She turned on a small radio. "Let's get some sounds going in here." Jared smiled and sat up on the sofa, folded the newspaper and followed Judy into the kitchen.

"Any good news today?" she asked, putting a few groceries away.

Jared stood across the room and dropped the newspaper on the table, watching Judy move back and forth, taking things out of her bag and stashing them into a cabinet. "About the usual. Jimmy Carter is going to fix the economy and we'll all live happily ever after. Neat, huh?"

Judy was facing the cabinet when Jared walked up to her. She could feel his breath on her neck. "Need any help, Judy?"

She let out a soft moan. "I think I've got it."

Jared's hands were on her hips, then her buttocks and back up again. She felt him cup both of her breasts, which were bra free. He moved his hands away under her T-shirt, stroking her smooth skin. His fingers caressed her nipples, and they grew hard.

Judy spun around and threw her arms around Jared's neck. Her kiss was warm and soft. She relaxed as he lifted her shirt up over her head and flung it onto the table. She stood still as he unhooked the snap to her cut offs and pulled them down, followed by the bikini bottom she wore under. She stepped clear of them.

"What about Dee? What if she walks in?"

"I'm not worried. She'll be a long time shopping for her momma."

Judy smiled and reached to put her arms around Jared's neck again. But he surprised her by bending down and grabbing her low and lifting her onto his shoulders.

"Oh, Jared. You caveman, you."

She rode on his shoulders as he carried her to DeeDee's room, slapping her ass as he went. The sting felt good to her.

"Oh, oh." Judy made soft cries pretending to be hurt by the slaps, but she couldn't keep from laughing. He dropped her onto her back on the bed, and she curled up into the fetal position, smiling at him. He stripped quickly and stood next to the bed, looking at her. Judy licked her index finger and then nudged his tip. As he grew, she slid her fingers around his part and guided him onto her. No need for other foreplay.

The couple lay on the bed and both fell into a slumber. When they awoke, she felt Jared's hands teasing her. She responded to his touch and her passion grew. He knelt beside her, smiling as she reached orgasm. Then he was in her again, thrusting rhythmically. They could hear the radio from the kitchen, but not the sound of DeeDee's car.

Chapter Forty-Two

I guess Leo thought it was funny that Wilkes wanted Fish to kill me, but I wasn't amused. I wanted to end the guy.

"Wilkes made it easy for us," said Leo, sitting in a chair near my desk. "He came right into the room and opened his big mouth."

I was about to say something clever to Leo when Millie Wallenski walked in.

"Excuse me, Detective, can I talk to you again?"

"Yes of course, Miss Wallenski." I turned to Leo and the others. "Give us a few minutes, will you?"

Agent Nelson looked agitated. As he started out of my office, I whispered to him. "This could be important. She works where Duarte was killed." He stopped just outside my door, but within earshot.

I motioned for her to sit in the chair just vacated by Leo. "What is it, Miss Wallenski?"

"Last night, I had a bad time with DeeDee, I mean really bad."

"Go ahead, explain. I'm listening."

"It was at the beginning of our shift. I went into the ladies room and DeeDee was there, standing at the sink and holding a kitchen knife. She was looking at it and crying and saying she never meant for this to happen. I don't know what she meant by that. I wanted to turn and leave, but she saw me. She grabbed the knife and pointed it at me and yelled, *What are you doing here? What are you doing here?*"

"Go on, Miss Wallenski. Then what happened?"

"She dropped the knife in the sink and came up to me. She grabbed my shoulders, hard, and then loosened up and said she was sorry, that she didn't mean to snap at me. I told her it was all right and that I figured she was still stressed out about Manny's death. I said he was such a good guy and we all missed him. That's when she looked at me kind of crazy like and said he wasn't such a good guy. When I asked what she meant, she said that Manny was related to a guy she had an affair with about ten months ago, a guy named Peter Duarte. A few weeks ago, Manny approached her and made remarks about Jared being a racist and how he'd be really pissed off if he ever learned about DeeDee's having sex with a Black guy."

"Slow down, Miss Wallenski. Can I get you some water?" I thought she was going to burst.

"No, no, I'm okay. So, Manny told DeeDee that he wanted her to have sex with him, or he'd tell Jared about her affair. DeeDee said she was terrified at what Jared might do and that she would lose him. She couldn't bear that, so she gave Manny what he wanted. She thought that was all that would happen, but Manny came back to her later and wanted it again. She refused, but was really scared. I asked her what happened and she said Manny must have lost his nerve, because Jared never said anything to her. Detective, I'm scared, too. When DeeDee pointed that knife at me, I didn't know what she was going to do. For a minute, she just seemed so crazy."

This story stunned me. It painted a whole new picture about what might have happened to Manny Duarte. Racism wasn't the only possible motive for his death. Jealousy and blackmail might also be involved, and a girl with a history of mental problems.

"Miss Wallenski, you did the right thing again by coming here and telling me this. DeeDee O'Hare committed an assault against you with a deadly weapon."

"Oh, no, really, she didn't mean it, I'm sure."

"Miss Wallenski, I want you to stay right in that chair and wait for a female officer. She's going to come in and ask you to tell her the whole story again. Just take your time and she'll write it all down for you to sign. I have to go with these other officers. We were just leaving when you arrived. Will you be okay?"

"Yes, I guess so. Yes, I will."

I left her with the female officer and told Leo, Jim and Agent Nelson what I had just heard. We had to move. I told Jim Pearson to contact Chief Wiley and have him come back to Dennis with an arrest team. We'll take Wilkes and hand him over to Chief Wiley. The FBI would move on WAR when Agent Nelson gave the green light.

"Get your guys ready, Jack," said Agent Nelson. "We take Wilkes now. Let's hope his nutty girlfriend doesn't make this complicated."

"They're ready to go," I said. "This time of day, he's probably at his girlfriend's house, but I'll send two cruisers over to The Chicken Roost, just in case he's there."

Agent Nelson and Leo rode with me while Jim Pearson and another uniformed officer followed. It was a long five-minute ride.

Jim and his partner parked a house away and approached on foot, covering the back. I gave them time to get in place before pulling up to the front of DeeDee O'Hare's place, blocking the cars in the driveway. We got out and had our weapons ready. I looked at Leo and Agent Nelson. Then all hell broke loose.

Judy Black came running out of the house through the front door, stark naked and screaming and with blood over her upper body. "Help me. Help me. She's going to kill me."

DeeDee O'Hare came running next, flashing a large kitchen knife. Leo stopped Judy and shielded her. I aimed at DeeDee and ordered her to halt. She stopped in her tracks, sobbing. "She wanted my Jared. She had no right. He's mine, forever. She'll never have him."

"Drop the knife, Miss O'Hare. Just drop it," I commanded.

"But she should be punished for what she did. She was in bed with Jared. I caught them. They were doing it right there in my bed. They didn't even hear me. But I heard them. I couldn't believe it. So, I got this and stopped them, for good."

I shot a look at Agent Nelson and Leo just as Jim Pearson appeared in the front door. "It's all over in here," he said. "Wilkes is dead in the bedroom. She slit his throat."

Leo got a blanket out of the car trunk and wrapped it around Judy Black, while I inched closer to DeeDee. I held up my hand to Jim and his partner who had their guns in hand.

"What happened, Miss O'Hare? Tell us what happened."

She held the knife with both hands, as if ready to thrust.

"I had to kill him, can't you see?"

"Why did you have to, Miss O'Hare?"

"I was so mad. I loved him and here he was screwing that bitch in my own bed. She ruined it all. Well, she can't have him. Nobody can. He belongs just to me."

"Yes, I guess that's right, Miss O'Hare. Now just let go of the knife. Let it drop. Nobody's going to hurt you."

People from other houses on the street had come out to see what was going on. They didn't dare come close.

Leo put Judy Black into the back seat of our car. Agent Nelson walked up beside me, his gun still in his hands. I hoped there wouldn't be reason to use it.

DeeDee stood there crying. "He shouldn't have done this to me. Jared loved me. I was going to stay here and work at the hospital, so we could always be together. He was for me, not for her. Why? Why?"

Jim moved closer to her. Finally, she lowered her arms and let the knife slip out of her hands. Jim grabbed her, pulling her hands behind her and cuffing her.

"Take her in your car, Jim, and read her rights. Radio in for an ambulance and the medical examiner."

The ride back to the station house was quiet. DeeDee O'Hare had composed herself and sat in a stunned silence. I was now certain that I knew what had happened to Manny Duarte, but I needed to have DeeDee confess.

Once we were back, DeeDee was booked, fingerprinted and told a public defender had been notified. I put her in the conference room with a female officer and readied myself for her interrogation. I was tempted to take a drink from a bourbon bottle I kept in my desk drawer, but thought the better of it. The last thing I needed was to have a defense lawyer smell liquor on my breath while questioning his client. A glass of water would have to do. I carried it into the conference room and sat down across the table from DeeDee.

"Hello, Detective," she said. "It's a rather nice day, don't you think?"

I glanced at Karen Orlando, the female officer. She returned my glance with a perplexed look.

"That depends on how you look at it, Miss O'Hare," I said.

"Why, what do you mean? The sun is out, the sky is blue and there's no humidity. I think it's perfect Cape weather, a great day for going to the beach. Do you go to the beach, Detective?"

You'd never guess that this woman had just slit a man's throat and attacked the girl he was in bed with.

"I mean that it's not a very pleasant day for Jared Wilkes."

"Oh, that. I don't want to talk about it."

I folded my hands on the table. "Well, aren't you lucky? You've been given your rights and you don't have to talk about Wilkes. That's okay, though, because I don't want to talk about him, either."

"You don't?" she said. "Then what on Earth do you want to talk to me about?"

"I want to talk about Manny Duarte."

"Oh, that bastard. I don't want to talk about him, either." The smile left her face.

"Yes, I want to talk about Manny Duarte, and his cousin, Peter Duarte."

DeeDee reached both hands onto the table and began tapping her fingers on it. "Peter, who's Peter? I don't know him."

"I think you do, Miss O'Hare. I think you knew him, all right. In fact, I believe you had a brief sexual affair with him several months ago."

She bit her lip, looked around the room, and focused for a moment on Officer Orlando, as if seeking support from another woman.

"You see, Miss O'Hare, I've had a couple of talks with Millie Wallenski, your waitress colleague. She told me about Peter. So, yes, you do know him."

"All right, so I know who he is. So what?" She continued tapping her fingers on the table. "I don't have to talk about it. You said I don't, and you can't ask me anymore."

"I said you don't have to talk about Jared Wilkes, and we're not. We're talking about Manny and Peter Duarte. You haven't been charged in Manny's case, so we can talk about that all we want. You know, Miss O'Hare, everybody says Manny was a prince of a guy. You're the only one who doesn't think so. Why is that, I wonder?"

"Because he was no fucking prince, that's why."

"But you had sex with him, didn't you, Miss O'Hare? You must have liked him a little bit, I'd say."

"No, I didn't like him. He was a bastard and I wouldn't give him the time of day."

"But you gave him much more than the time, didn't you? You gave him what he wanted."

"No, no, I didn't GIVE him anything. He took it. He took it from me."

"Yes, Miss O'Hare, he took it from you." I took a drink of water. "But once wasn't enough for him, was it?"

"No, that goddamned son of a bitch. He kept taking. Three times, goddamn it, three times and he wanted more. He wanted to own me."

DeeDee stopped talking. I motioned to Officer Orlando to get a glass of water for her. I drank more from my cup and, when Orlando returned, DeeDee gulped some of hers.

"Go on, Miss O'Hare. Go on."

"He was going to ruin it, don't you see?"

"Ruin what?" I asked.

"Why, me and Jared, of course. I was in love with him and he loved me. He said he did. I was going to make Jared happy forever. But Manny was going to ruin it. He was going to tell Jared about me and Peter. I couldn't let that happen. Jared hates Black people. If he knew I had sex with a Black man, Jared would have been furious with me. He would have broken up with me, for sure. I couldn't stand that. I couldn't live without Jared. I had to stop Manny."

"How could you do that, Miss O'Hare? Manny was a strong young man. How could you stop him?"

"That was easy. Manny and I worked at the same restaurant. I remembered the murder in Needham last fall. It was in the papers. Somebody hid in a guy's car outside of a restaurant and when the guy came out and got back in his car, the killer slashed his throat from behind."

"So that's what you did to Manny?"

"Of course. It was so easy. He never even knew I was in his car. He started the engine and I slit his throat. All I had to do was slip out of the car on the other side and duck away through the bushes. I ran back to my car parked up the street, drove to the beach and threw the knife into the water. I didn't even get any blood on me, but I washed my hands later, just in case. It was SO easy."

"You're right about one thing, Miss O'Hare. Manny was no prince."

"You understand, then, Detective, why I had to do it."

I motioned to Officer Orlando. She left the room briefly and returned with Sergeant Pearson.

"And you understand, Miss O'Hare, that you are now also under arrest for the murder of Manny Duarte?" I gave her rights once again. She sat quietly, a slight smile across her lips, as if her explanation to me made everything okay.

I went out to my office area where Leo and Agent Nelson were waiting and I explained what had just happened.

"Good job today, Jack. You caught three killers, Fish, Wilkes and this O'Hare girl," said Agent Nelson.

"But we've lost a witness against WAR."

"Wilkes has already given us enough on them. We can shut them down. Davey Esteban's testimony will give us plenty on Sammy White: extortion, assault, and racketeering. We need Agent Watson. I hope she has enough for us to get Tommy Shea and his boys, too. I'm going to give her another day. But I don't want to wait anymore for going after those creeps at WAR. I'm calling for warrants right away."

"Chief Wiley will be glad to hear that. He lost a good young officer to those racist bastards. If you have your team coordinate with Wiley, I can meet you in Marshfield."

"Don't you have enough on your hands here? You don't have to go with us to Marshfield."

"Those guys, or more likely Sammy White working with them, put a hit out on me. I want to see that asshole Holiday's face when I show up. He doesn't know me, so I'll be glad to introduce myself. If he gives us White, we're that much closer to Tommy Shea."

"Okay, Jack. I guess you're in the party."

"Leo, too," I said. "He kept surveillance on their headquarters. He deserves to get a shot in this."

Agent Nelson didn't argue the point. We agreed to meet at Marshfield Police Headquarters. I told Leo the good news.

Chapter Forty-Three

By four o'clock we met in Marshfield with Agent Nelson, his FBI team of thirty agents and Chief Wiley. His men would provide back up for the FBI, but would not engage unless so ordered. This was an FBI show and Leo and I had guest passes.

We followed five FBI vans to the entrance driveway to WAR's building. The Marshfield PD sealed off the driveway once we were on the property. Thirty agents dressed in riot gear and carrying assault rifles surrounded the building. Once they were in place, Agent Nelson used a bullhorn to announce his presence.

"This is the FBI. Your building is surrounded. Come out peacefully with your hands behind your neck. If you do not comply, we will use force to take the building." As he spoke, several agents approached the building, taking up positions near the front door and windows. After ten seconds, Agent Nelson repeated his commands.

About five seconds went by when a voice called out. "Okay. I'm coming out."

The front door swung opened and two figures emerged, their hands positioned as ordered. One was a young guy, about five-ten, wearing jeans rolled up at the cuff over Doc Martin motorcycle boots and a red T-shirt. Behind came a man in his thirties wearing a mod-looking suit and no neck tie. Agents were on them in a flash, handcuffing them behind their backs. They offered no resistance. Other agents sprang into the building, their weapons ready.

"Which one of you is Wilfred Holiday?" asked Agent Nelson.

"Really now," said the guy in the mod suit. "Does he look like a Wilfred Holiday to you?" He nodded toward the red shirt guy.

"You're under arrest for conspiracy to murder a Federal agent. We'll start with that. The Marshfield PD also will have charges against you in the murder of Officer Angela Green." Agent Nelson read him his rights.

I holstered my weapon and walked up close to Holiday. "My name is Detective Jack Contino, the guy you wanted killed. Only your man Wilkes wasn't up to the task."

Holiday looked stoic.

"Well, you're a rather large fellow, now, ain't you? Might want to go on a diet, Jack. You don't want to die of a heart attack, now, do you?"

We heard the sound of boots against the floor inside and some file cabinets being opened and closed. There was a lot of fire power around and inside the building, but not a shot was fired. An agent came out through the front door. "The place is empty, sir. Nobody else inside and the cabinets are clean. Just a few swastikas on the wall, a WAR banner and a big picture of Hitler."

"All right," said Nelson. "Take these guys away."

I looked at Leo and then at Nelson. "Almost like they were ready for this."

"Yeah, kind of strange," said Leo.

"Maybe not," I said. "Maybe they're better organized than we thought. They don't let too many people in here at one time. They might have just cleaned out the files, so check the cars. They might have stashed some things in the trunk for a fast move."

"Well, we've definitely got Wilkes on tape about the hit on Officer Green and the contract on Jack," said Leo.

"But unless Holiday talks, we've got nothing connecting them to Shea," said Agent Nelson. "We're really counting on Agent Watson now."

"Holiday doesn't strike me as the deal-making kind of guy," I said. "As for Agent Watson, I've got a bad feeling about her."

"I still want to wait until tomorrow to move against White. I want to give her a chance to help us nail Shea. If I don't hear from her, we'll pick up White based on Davey Esteban's testimony."

"That reminds me," said Leo. "I'm hungry. Let's get a pizza."

Chapter Forty-Four

The following day I went home after work, not hearing anything from the FBI. I poured myself a bourbon while Natalie started fixing dinner. I wasn't being good company, so she gave me some space.

I was on my second drink when the phone rang. Natalie answered it in the kitchen. "Oh, hello, Agent Nelson. Yes, he's here. Hold on a minute."

I took the call in the living room. I wiped my palms on my pants before lifting the receiver. "Hello, Agent Nelson."

"Jack, I've got some good news and some bad news. What'll it be?"

"Let's start with the good."

"Got it. We took Sal DiFino, aka Sammy White, today. He was at his own house in Somerville this morning. He didn't put up a struggle, played it pretty cool. We tried to interview him at headquarters, but he went silent. His lawyer got there in about an hour."

"Was Agent Watson there?"

"No, I'm afraid not. That's part of the bad news. Her belongings were there, including her badge and her weapon. So you may have been right about her all along, Jack. She didn't hide the fact from DiFino that she was FBI. She must have been working it both ways."

"She was shacking up with DiFino, definitely crossing the line. But things were starting to go bad for her. That's why she told me about DiFino ranting about the WAR guys and how he was going to get me. What about her apartment?"

"No sign of her there and she hasn't called in yet. It's not looking good."

"What about Shea?"

"Nothing we can do there except put some heat on and see what he does. Unless DiFino or Holiday give him up, we've got nothing on him."

"Damn. Maybe Leo and I can help find Agent Watson. We still have some good contacts in Somerville and . . ."

"Jack, slow down. You're supposed to be semi-retired on the Cape. You really stuck your neck out on this one and it helped us, but you need to focus on Dennis PD business. You solved your Manny Duarte case and helped us get Fish and Wilkes for the Officer Green killing. WAR is shut down and we've got their leader. It's time for you to kick back and relax."

"I appreciate that, Agent Nelson, but I can't relax completely as long as Tommy Shea is walking free."

"I know, Jack. Look, with Holiday and DiFino, I think we'll get to Shea somehow. And I have to hope that Agent Watson will have something for us to use against Shea. You've done your job and more, Jack. I personally want to thank you for that."

"That goes both ways. But be sure to call me when you've got some news, just to keep me informed. I promise not to beat a path to your office."

"Understood, Jack. Now go hug your wife and tell her what I just said. Bye, Jack."

Nat was standing near the kitchen table when I went to her. I did what Agent Nelson said. The hug did us both good.

The End

About the Author

Steve Marini holds a Master's degree in Educational Technology from Boston University and a B.A. in Business Administration from New England College and has spent over thirty years in the Education/Training field, including posts in higher education and the federal government.

Although he describes himself as a "card carrying New Englander," he lived for twenty-six years in Maryland while pursuing a career spanning four federal agencies. His background has enabled him to serve as a project manager at the National Security Agency, the Environmental Protection Agency, the National Fire Academy and the Centers for Medicare and Medicaid Services, where he worked with teams of experts in various fields to develop state-of-the-art training for both classrooms and distance learning technologies.

A "Baby Boomer," Steve has taken up fiction writing as he moved into his career final frontier. Married for thirty-six years, a father of three and a grandfather, Steve and his wife Louise own a home on Cape Cod that will serve as his private writer's colony for the years ahead.

BLOG: http://babyboomerspm.blogspot.com/
FACEBOOK: http://www.facebook.com/StevenPMarini